Praise for YELLOWCA[KE]

★ "Haunting, gorgeous, and sometimes painful, Lanagan's stories are unlike anything else in fantasy literature."   —*Publishers Weekly*, Starred

"Lanagan's literary chops are nearly unrivaled in YA lit, and any release from her will draw excitement, scrutiny, and awards consideration . . . lovely, enigmatic, and eye-opening."   —*Booklist*

"Lanagan's prose is challenging and rewarding in equal measure, creating resonances that most writers can only dream of; and her characters and situations seethe with emotional power."   —*VOYA*

★ "Stunning. . . . A good introduction to Lanagan's mind-bending work."
—*Kirkus Reviews*, Starred

"In all of Lanagan's worlds, the familiar becomes unfamiliar and then wondrous."   —*School Library Journal*

"Unsettling, startling, often gruesome—these imaginative works demand much of their readers, occasionally providing catharsis and unfailingly provoking thought and discussion."   —*The Horn Book*

Also by Margo Lanagan

*The Brides of Rollrock Island*

*Tender Morsels*

*Red Spikes*

*Black Juice*

*White Time*

# Yellowcake

stories

## MARGO LANAGAN

WITHDRAWN

EMBER

Text copyright © 2006, 2008, 2009, 2011, 2013 by Margo Lanagan
Cover photograph copyright © 2013 by Yolande de Kort/Trevillion Images

All rights reserved. Published in the United States by Ember, an imprint of Random House Children's Books, a division of Random House LLC, a Penguin Random House Company, New York. Collection originally published by Alfred A. Knopf, an imprint of Random House Children's Books, New York, in 2013. The stories in this collection, with the exception of "Into the Clouds on High," were originally published between 2006 and 2011 in a variety of publications. For a full account of the publication history, please refer to the author's note at the back of the book.

Ember and the E colophon are registered trademarks of Random House LLC.

Visit us on the Web! randomhouse.com/teens

Educators and librarians, for a variety of teaching tools, visit us at RHTeachersLibrarians.com

The Library of Congress has cataloged the hardcover edition of this work as follows:
Lanagan, Margo
Yellowcake : stories / Margo Lanagan.
p. cm.
First published: Australia : Allen & Unwin Publishers, 2011.
Summary: A collection of ten short stories of unusual people, places, and events, including reimagined classic tales and original works, most of which were previously published.
Contents: The point of roses—The golden shroud—A fine magic—An honest day's work—Into the clouds on high—Night of the firstlings—Catastrophic disruption of the head—Ferryman—Living curiosities—Eyelids of the dawn.
ISBN 978-0-375-86920-4 (trade) — ISBN 978-0-375-96920-1 (lib. bdg.) —
ISBN 978-0-375-98931-5 (ebook) — ISBN 978-0-375-87335-5 (pbk.)
[1. Short stories.] I. Title. II. Title: Yellow cake.
PZ7.L216Yel 2013 [Fic]—dc23 2012013139

Printed in the United States of America
10 9 8 7 6 5 4 3 2 1
First Ember Edition 2015

# Contents

The Point of Roses . . . 1

The Golden Shroud . . . 29

A Fine Magic . . . 45

An Honest Day's Work . . . 59

Into the Clouds on High . . . 87

Night of the Firstlings . . . 111

Catastrophic Disruption of the Head . . . 127

Ferryman . . . 163

Living Curiosities . . . 175

Eyelids of the Dawn . . . 195

# Yellowcake

# The Point of Roses

Billy flew into the kitchen. The screen door clapped closed after him.

"You're back," said Nance.

Corin looked up from the dishes, to the world reflected in the window. The boy was wild and clammy-looking from running, his clothes every which way and filthy, his chest going with his panting. Nance admired him as he passed.

"Just for a minute," he said. "I've got to fetch some stuff."

"What stuff? For what?" barked Corin automatically.

"Just stuff. Any old thing. Three things." This last was tossed back from halfway down the hall.

The boy rummaged in his room, and rattled. Then he was back in the doorway.

"You need a haircut," said Corin to the boy's reflection.

"What are you wild lads up to?" said Nance.

"Shai's brother's got psychic powers. We're doing experiments."

"Psychic powers! Well, well," said Nance.

"Maybe he can tell you where you dropped that shed key," said Corin.

"Not that kind of power," said Billy scornfully.

"Of course, not anything *useful*."

There was a skillful summoning whistle outside.

"I've got to go," said Billy, starting for the door.

"Kiss!" Nance commanded.

He darted back, kissed her cheek quickly and was gone.

Corin was up to his elbows in suds. Nance, at the table in her glasses, went slowly on through the newspaper. She would suck up all the news, but she would never speak to him about it, as if he didn't have ears or something. As if he didn't have a brain to hear with. As if he might not *like* to hear, because reading it himself was such a labor.

"What's the boy got there?" said Corin, putting his forehead to the window. He brought sudsy hands up to block out the other reflections.

"He's got . . ." Nance looked up and dredged the picture of Billy out of her memory. "He's got Pumfter von Schnitzel, and that ashtray. The one on a stick."

Ah yes, from the old days, when Corin had pleased himself where he smoked. "And he's pinched one of those blessed roses on the way out," Corin said. "The Zephyr ones. Or whatever silly name they've got."

Nance licked her fingertip and caught up a corner of the paper. "Hmm," she said, reading.

Corin looked over his shoulder at her. "You're not bothered?"

"Bothered by the rose? He can have a rose. As long as he's not tearing the petals off every bloom."

"By any of those things. What if he loses that dog thing?"

She looked up at him, dragging her mind back from wherever to hear him. "He doesn't need it as much as he used to."

"You said you'd never find another with quite such a look on its face. You said in the whole basket there were no others with that look. It's an accident, the way his eyes were sewn on."

"What a memory. That was years ago." Nance looked properly at him now. "You just don't want him playing with those Traveller kids."

"My eye, I don't."

"You're not really so bothered about Pumfter."

"Maybe not."

Nance went back to the paper.

Corin sudsed on; plates clanked in the sink and then clacked into the rack. He heard his breath adjusting itself to every shift of his anxiety.

"It's nearly *dark*," he said.

"It's summer," said Nance in that *patient* tone he hated. "It's long evenings. You go out there and let your eyes adjust and see how dark it is."

"Maybe I should. Maybe I should follow the little bugger and see what they're up to."

"Maybe." There she went again. What she meant was, *Of course you shouldn't! Leave the boy to his adventures, you clumsy great berk.*

Corin heaved a sigh. He sneaked a look at Nance's reflection. Was she smiling? He wouldn't put it past her, to have a smile at his expense. Smug cow.

"Where is he, then?" asked Billy.

"Up on the hill in the reserve," said Shai. "We'll go up and signal when we're near."

"He can't spy down on us and see?"

"It's all bushy. And he doesn't *want* to cheat, remember. Besides, he'd never guess *this*. What is it?"

"It's an ashtray."

"Like, for smoking?" Shai looked it up and down. "It's huge."

"You stand it, beside your armchair." Billy stood it in the air as they walked. "Then you tap-tap your ash on the little tray there and *push* the button, and it spins and all goes in underneath, see?"

"It's a marvel. What a thing. Well, I know Jo's never seen such a one. And a toy, there."

"It's supposed to be a dog." Billy held Pumfter up and watched him do his work on Shai's face.

"That's got a friendly look. Let me hold him a second—ooh, his flower came away."

"That's the third thing. It's a rose. My grandma grows them and they win prizes."

6

"I thought it were part of the doggy. You were very pretty with your rose, weren't you, doggy? He's a good size. For holding, eh. Or for tucking away here, look. I can carry him?"

"Of course you can. I've got to keep this rose nice. And manage this ashtray, or it'll trip me up. Have we got to go through bushes or anything?"

"We can go around by the walking path. But we've to pick up Castle and Alex first."

"No, you've not." Their two forms bobbed darkly up out of the hedge.

"You must have shoveled that dinner," said Shai.

"We did. Dad said it was disgusting. Alex's made himself sick."

"Don't talk about it," said Alex. "I'll keep it down if I think of something else."

"He wouldn't miss this, not after I told him about last time," said Castle to Shai.

"Hopefully, we won't get into such trouble," said Shai. "Hopefully, we're far enough away."

"In Cottinden's Domain? It's a bloody hike, all right. It'll be dead dark coming home."

"It'll be worth it. And there'll be a moon."

By the time they got to the hilltop, Billy was just about puffed. No one had helped him with the long-stemmed ashtray or the fragile rose, although Pumfter von Schnitzel had been passed

7

from boy to boy all the way. He was now in Alex's shirt, his kind face poking out between buttons. *It's all right*, he seemed to say to Billy. *None of them are clean, but you can wash me, remember? Just throw me in the machine.*

Jo was idling on the picnic table at the hilltop. Trees crowded behind him. The pinking light in their upper branches glowed also in the pale, grubby cloth of Jo's shirt.

Shai gave his whistle and Jo came alert and called out, in Travellers' language, and Shai called back.

"And bnah bnah blah blah Billy?" said Jo.

"He's here."

To Billy it was a marvel, that they could switch between one language and another. And a shame and an honor both, that they would stay in his language while he was with them.

"You're set?" Shai called out.

"It's not a matter of *me* being set." Jo's face moved against the dark trees, searching for some sight of them.

"Well, we've got everything. You can start any time."

"You got three things?"

"Aye."

"Choose one, then. Put it forward of you, and keep the others back. Behind a stone or a big tree or something."

Alex scrabbled Pumfter out of his shirt. The boys all looked to Billy.

"No," said Billy. "Let's put this flower first, before it spoils or gets stepped on or something."

"Here." Shai ushered him toward a boulder covered with

picnickers' graffiti. "INDIA 4 STORM—remember that. Put the others behind there."

"Why?" Billy laid Pumfter down and propped the ashtray against some stones so that it wouldn't roll. "I mean, why remember? We'll be right here, won't we?"

"Maybe not. There might be a bit of traveling involved. A bit of wandering."

"Oh." Billy had thought it would be more like a show, where they sat and rested and watched.

"So. Put that forward on the ground there. But not anywhere Jo can see it."

"I can't see nothing in those bushes," said Jo. "I'm not even trying."

"It's forward. We're ready," said Shai. "Do your thing."

"Yer, shake yer booty," said Castle.

"Ah, shhh!" said Shai. "You've got to be serious."

"I can't help it. It's funny."

"You spoil this, I'll whack you so hard," hissed Alex.

"Quiet in there, then," said Jo from the clearing. "I can't go with all that racket."

"Can't go? What's he doing, working up a good crap? Ow."

"Shut up, you meelmeek."

"All right, I'm going," Jo sang out.

"Where to, is he going?" Billy murmured to Shai.

"Off away to the inside of his own head," said Shai. "He's got to use the psychic place. It's right in the middle, he says. In his lizard brain."

They waited. For quite some minutes they were four boys crouched in bushes, one boy on a picnic table, and a fragrant rose in between. Evening hung above them, its high, cool note singing on and on over the crickets' pulsing. Birds flew home and put themselves to bed here and there. Some land creature moved, Billy couldn't tell how far away, or what size, shrew or badger or wandering pony.

Then Jo got up and, with fluid movements that were not his own, stepped from table to bench to ground. He groped at the two buttons of his pinkish-whitish shirt, undid them by hauling rather than finger work, dragged the shirt off over his head and stood there frowning, swinging his face blindly.

" 'S around here somewhere," he said in a deep, drugged voice.

He lifted his face to listen. Rose-ness welled up out of the evening and rushed at them. Alex gave a shout. A sweet-scented shock hit Billy, a velvety punch. Down the slope he tumbled, alone in a storm of blooms, streaked and scraped with darker leaves. His lungs struggled, his skin dissolved, his thoughts turned to vapor as the rose essence passed through, roaring.

Corin was at the bins. He felt it coming as you feel a wave in the sea; it sucked stuff away, ahead of itself. Corin gripped the rim of the council wheelie bin, tried to stand firmer on the bumpy ground of the bin yard.

It hit, a powerful buffet of sweet air. It tossed his hair, rocked him, rocked the near-full bin. It must have rocked the roses. It must have stripped Nance's roses from their stems, to carry such a scent.

But there were no petals on the streaming air. Corin ran against the wind, blundered out of the yard and around the house. He must see what had happened.

At the corner of the house, the wind stopped him, like a rose-scented tarpaulin stretched across his path. But only he was blown and bewildered; nothing else moved, not a twig, not a leaf, not a flower. All Nance's garden stood serene in the dying summer evening.

But along the fence the rosebushes were jagged black candelabra. The roses brightened in the bloom wind, the rose wind, big soft rose-lamps propped among the rough leaves and the thorns. They shone and they shed—was it a smoke? It was like dust, or tiny seeds, or tiny, numerous, distant stars gone to milk in the sky, or like the curls of grainy steam from your soup or your tea. This stuff purled and streamered across the lawn to Corin; he breathed it and it filled his brain, which had broken open when the wind first hit him.

*Her* name *is Rose*, he thought dizzily, and knew he had hit upon something.

Nostrils flared, mouth wide to keep catching the wind, he stumbled after the strand of thought, back along the house wall.

He saw Nance through the screen. The white tail of her hair was blown forward over one shoulder; hair wisps danced around her face, which was all opened out and smoothed of its lines and thoughts by surprise. The newspaper lay flat on the kitchen table where Nance had pushed it back; it was unmoved by the wind. But the rose catalogue that had been underneath—Nance held some of the catalogue pages down, but others rattled back and forth in the breeze, and the photographed roses were smudged on the pages, and shed sweet crimson, velvet mauve and soft ivory across the kitchen air.

"Rose!" He called her true name through the screen. Because—he would never be able to explain to her!—she was the source of it. It was she who blew the rose coals to brightness, it was she who, in the first place, had had the idea of the roses. It was she—it was the children all over again! He saw that, too! He had fumed and raged against each pregnancy, and snarled and boiled and beat at the children as they grew, and railed at her for enslaving herself to them, instead of to him! But there she'd been, swelling and dreaming and knitting and working and reading to them and making their little foods and fending him off them, all according to the garden plan in her head. She had had the children plotted out just so, as if on sheets of squared paper, and she had kept him out, just as she'd not let him do a spadeful of digging or bring a barrowload of bricks to edge the rose bed—because he snarled and sneered so, because, allowed in, his anger would have thrashed about and damaged the whole project of the roses, of the children, of the garden.

"I'm sorry about the roses!" He felt as if he shouted, but it came out a child's cry, afraid the night would hear and descend on him. The wind softened; the rose colors were fading in the kitchen; Nance's hair settled and she looked about, for herself and for him, the speaker beyond the door screen.

"It just seemed so old-womanish," he said falteringly, trying to get *some* words out before the wind, the thought, entirely went. "I just wanted you to stay my girl—"

And it was gone. The last colors slid off the catalogue pages and trickled to invisibility across the table.

Nance stood up and scraped the chair back. "Of course!" She came around to the door. She was laughing, but not unkindly. "So that you could stay a boy, and all the girls still want you! Well, what kind of life is that, on and on and on? What is the use of that?"

"I don't know," he said, frightened. "But I didn't know . . . what was the use of roses, either. I couldn't see the point before, you see—"

She pressed her mouth to the screen, and he met it with his. Their warmths warmed the mesh. She put her hand up beside her face, and he matched it with his hand, and they were there for a moment, like reflections of each other, yet quite different. Quite different from each other, yet meeting at the mouth.

The other boys talked in Traveller, bubbles and scraps of noise. Billy lay on the hillside, gripping the ground with his hands, with the skin of his back, with the back of his head. Above him everything swirled in the aftermath, and a few stars sang, restoring the world to stillness.

"Hum-humnah-Billy?"

"Wait," he said sharply.

"Oof. Arf," said Castle. "I'm all gone to petals and come back again."

*Yes,* thought Billy, *they're about the words for it.*

"How does Jo go?" he said. It was hard to shape his mouth around all that meaning.

"Me?" said Jo, in his normal voice. "I'm all right. I'm *very* all right. Don't worry about me."

"It makes him feel good," said Shai. "It gives him jollies. He'll be impossible, these next few days."

Jo clapped and rubbed his hands. Both sounds seemed to happen right inside Billy's head. "So what else have you got for me?" he said.

"What was that one, first?" said Castle.

" 'Twas a rose. An old Bourbon rose called Zéphirine Drouhin, soft midpink in color, with a strong fragrance. A little fussy in its habits and prone to black spot. The absence of thorns makes this rose ideal for children's play areas, and—"

"All right, give it a rest," said Shai. "Get back on your table."

"No, I'm down now. I'm ambillant. I'm good."

"Well, turn around, then."

"I tell you, I can't see. It's like a black curtain—well, dark gray, with branches and trunks."

"Turn around so *we* know. This is a scientific test."

"Sheesh, can we wait a bit?" muttered Alex in a mooshed voice. He must have had his face in his hands.

"Not too long," said Shai. "He's on his roll now. Billy, get that rose back and put out the next object."

Billy pushed the spinning part of his brain into a corner. He bent and retrieved the rose from the bushes. He sniffed deeply of it as he took it to the INDIA 4 STORM rock, but no, it was only the merest hint of the rose-ness that had passed over and through him. It was nearly nothing in comparison, yet it was something enough to send him mad with sniffing and trying and yearning, if he let it.

Pumfter regarded him kindly, and he patted the dog's worn cloth head. Then he laid the rose beside Pumfter and took out the ashtray.

It tinked and rattled as he pushed it into the bush.

"It's a cowbell; that was easy," said Jo.

"Don't be cheeky," said Shai.

Jo paced back and forth. His chest was narrow and bruised-looking. "Are we ready, then? Are we good?"

"Shut up, Jo. Alex, how are you coming?"

"I'm a bit better."

"What about you, Billy?"

"I'll be all right," said Billy stoutly.

"Right, Jo. We're ready for you."

A jittery silence fell. The forest sounds flowed into it.

Jo stood poised, as if about to take a step, or to bend forward and vomit.

"Gawd," said Castle under his breath, "what will he make of *this*?"

"He doesn't *make* anything," said Shai. "He told me. He just connects. The object uses him to find, I dunno, something else. Something bigger. Oops—"

Jo had swung away from them, had started down the far slope.

"Quick, after him!" said Shai. "Sometimes he whistles along. Billy, you bring the object."

Billy caught up with them at the forest edge. Jo moved on ahead, indistinct as a marsh candle, as quietly as if he were flowing around the trees, floating over the ground, and the others thudded after him, grunting and swearing.

"Where is the bugger?" said Shai. "I've lost him."

"Down there," said Billy. "Headed for the brook. See?"

"Good man."

When they reached Jo, he had dropped his pants and belt on the thin crescent of sand. He stood up to his calves in the shallows of a pool, which a lacework of tiny waterfalls spilled into. A star reflection rocked jauntily over the ripples he made.

"Watch him," whispered Shai. "He can't swim. When he's like this, he thinks he can, though. Fly, too, sometimes."

Jo stood, bent as if cold, his hands dark on his knees. He turned and looked straight at them, his face skull-like and awful in the darkness. "Shhhh," he said.

"Think about the thing, the object!" said Shai in a terrified whisper.

Billy locked his mind onto the image of a younger, red-haired Grandpa Corin. This Corin laid his cigarette in the ashtray, ignoring the fascinated Billy at his knee. He resettled his bum in the big armchair, hunched over the form guide. The cigarette smoke went up in straight lines to a certain level, then began to bend and twine. The tiny Billy itched, stuffed full of one desire: *Press the button, Grandpa. Spin it away. Before Nance comes and finds me and snatches me up, and says, "Come away from that dirty thing. Leave your Grandpa to his smells, why don't you"*—

Jo straightened, and reached his skinny arms up, and spread his fingers, and gathered something down on himself, down on them all. It blotted out the sky in an instant. It crushed the boys flat to the ground, and filled their minds and mouths with ashes.


Corin pushed Nance away.

"It's coming again!" He tried to see it beyond the walls of the bright kitchen.

"You think?" said Nance hopefully. Her lips were pinked from kissing him. Her whole face had come unset from its folds and habits; from here it might age any number of different ways.

"It's at Cowper Fen with the Travellers now." Fearfully Corin searched the ceiling. "Though it's not from there; it's from beyond there. It's wobbling the church steeple! It'll be here soon, it'll be in the garden!—"

A cindery blast pushed him against the cupboards and the door. Who was he? Who was that old lady, clutching the table edge? She was someone's grandmother; she had one of those strong, capable, sexless bodies in the middle of all those wind-whipped clothes. But she would die anyway; he knew it.

He was running in the night. Things banged and obstructed his knees; things shattered in his wake. Tiny cries came after him. "Don't call out like that!" he muttered. "Don't go right back to a *baby*!"

The bin-yard wall caught him in the ribs, smacked the breath out of him, lashed his head forward. The ground lit up orange. Hot air attacked his face, swooped down his throat and choked him.

The yard was a pit, full of magma that turned and split and sank into itself. In the time before the electric, Corin had gathered and stamped years' worth of ashes, to make the yard floor; now these had all come alive again, and stank, and melted. The plastic bins drooped, and the raised letters on the council bin—NO HOT ASHES—glowed in the moments before the bin collapsed and was enfolded. Flames came and went across the mass, like runners of grass, only of fire.

Corin hung coughing, aghast, over the wall. New knowledge bounded through him, like a herd of black bulls caught along a narrow street and panicking: this ashy wind that pinned him here, it went nowhere; it blew only from one giant hollowness to another. He, Rose, everyone they knew, everyone they had ever known, every *thing*—put together, they were no more than one of those white sparks, there for a moment on the breast of the turning magma, and then engulfed and gone utterly.

"Corin! Corin!" she cried from the house. At any other time it would have started him running, it would have flicked him like a switch it was so raw, so full of fear and sorrow, so unlike the Nance he knew and wanted, the Nance he relied on to take the brunt of him. But now, with fumes in his eyes and the fire bawling and stretching and being consumed below him—*What can she do for me? Or I for her? All we can do is scrabble at each other, moan our fear at each other as we go down.*

Afterward, Nance found him crouched by the wall, staring unblinking at the new-risen moon, coated like herself in the finest of fine gray ash.

"That's an ashtray, that one," said Jo cheerily. "Made of chrome-plated steel. A mechanism, activated by a Bakelite knob, spins the ash and cigarette butts into the bulb below, where any remaining spark is extinguished by oxygen starvation."

"Mechanism," said Shai through chattering teeth. "*Extinguished*. He don't get those words from our family."

Billy didn't know how Shai could talk at all. Billy himself had died just now; he had felt himself choking, and death had twirled his brain out of his head and mulched it into some substance that would be used again and again, to make ants or trees, or maybe other people, or maybe gases for some other planet, and all Billy-ness had left the world forever.

Now here he was, back, boy in wood, so frightened he didn't know how he was going to get home to Nance and Grandpa Corin's. Jo was cackling and prancing naked in the shallows;

the others were huddled around Billy, all warmth and gulping breath. Alex's ear was pearly and intricate in the faint light; the very grubbiness of the hand, the very bitten-ness of the nails that came up to scratch it made Billy feel weepy and full of wonder. At the same time, he held in his guts a black cannonball of fear; it sat and sucked all possible movement out of his body.

"Come on, you." Jo capered around them, scattering cold drops of brook water. "One more!"

"Put your clothes on, you geet," growled Castle. "You look like a death doll, all head and willy."

Jo laughed insanely and danced off to obey.

The four others risked looking at each other. *Thank heaven*, thought Billy. He had thought his own face must be peeled back to the skull; now he knew, seeing Castle's wary eyes and Alex's teary ones, that he looked like his old, young self.

"That was *horrible*!" whimpered Alex, and a hiccuping breath made the juices rattle in his nose.

"I'm sorry," said Billy. "The ashtray was a bad idea. But I used to *like* it. You said—" He turned to Shai. "You said, pick things that *mean* something. So I did. I didn't know it would—" He broke off so as not to cry, waving his hands about.

"It's all right," said Shai. "You weren't to know. How were you to know? Who'd have thought *that*, of an ashtray? My oath."

They all four turned. Jo was trying to put his second leg in his shorts; he hopped sideways on the sand, bent headless over the task. Castle shuddered and turned away.

"I don't want to do another one," said Alex. "I just want

to be at home. But I don't want to walk home through this forest—it's all shadows and noises."

"Well, you'll have to, won't you?" snapped Castle.

Billy felt the same as Alex. What were they going to do? he wondered.

"Wait a bit," said Shai, patting Alex's shoulder. "Let it fade a bit."

"It'll *never* fade," Alex whispered. "I'll *never* forget."

"You will, too," said Shai. "Just like you forget a bad dream."

"I don't forget those, either," said Alex, weeping. "I lie there going over and over it in my head, and trying not to go back to sleep and have it again. And sometimes I *do* go to sleep, and I *do* have it again—"

"Shut up or I'll slap you, Alex," said Castle. "You're working yourself up. Now stop it."

Alex stopped, and mopped his eyes miserably.

"Look," said Shai. "The moon's coming up. That'll be daylight, practically."

*Except that moon shadows are blacker than sun ones,* thought Billy. *They can hide more things, to jump out at you.* But he didn't say it; he wasn't about to frighten himself worse.

Nance went to Corin through the broken flowerpots. He was against a wall, and beyond the wall was the grave—she smelled its greasy sweetness. He was all bones wrapped thinly in flesh, then loosely in cloth; his hair was white scraps floating from his speckled scalp in the moonlight.

"Come inside, Corin," she scolded in her crone's voice. "Look at you! You're all over ashes!" How had they got to be so old, she and he? It seemed to Nance that they had held each other in a death clasp all these years, meanly squeezing until every scrap of color was gone from skin and hair, until their voices held no juice and their eyes too much. It seemed a dreadful desperate together-ness, this marriage, quite biological and loveless; she had watched frogs mating once, and it was like that, like a long, hard clinch with spasms of wrestling, now sinking, now floating, and all the while the eyes looking out, frog eyes, showing nothing. And here she was, kicking shards out of the way with her frog feet, and shaking the ash off his shirt with her frog hands—no, with her old-woman's hands, all worn and creased—whoever would have thought moonlight could be so cruel? Look at them! She snatched them off him and hid them from herself.

She reached for something habitual to say. "I'll run you a bath," she brayed at him. "Corin?"

He would not look up. She crouched in front of him, leaning against the tomb wall.

"Corin. Corin."

The moonlight gave him a great and glowing brow. His eye-brows sizzled along its rim. The bulls thundered from his skull holes into hers, on and on. She could do nothing, for herself or for him; she couldn't even blink. His eyes' black beams had caught and locked her.

\*  \*  \*

Slowly, carefully, chivied by jolly Jo, keeping hold of each other's shirts and elbows, and Alex and Castle holding hands because they were brothers and that was all right, they crept back up the hill. Billy kept himself going by thinking: *As soon as I'm up top, I'll tell them, No more. I'll take Pumfter and I'll go home. No, I'll leave Pumfter. They can do what they want with him; they can bring him back to me tomorrow.*

They reached the clearing. Jo climbed up and sat cross-legged on the table, grinning in the moonlight.

"Don't be *creepy*," said Castle.

"Fetch the last one. Go on. I'm readier than ready."

"That's obvious."

Billy didn't feel so bad after the climb. And now he didn't fancy going home on his own, so much. So he went with Shai to the INDIA 4 STORM rock.

Shai picked Pumfter up and hugged him. Billy had to stop himself snatching at the dog: That's *mine*! His rage was like the stiffness that happened in his throat when he was about to be sick; he swallowed down hard on it, and laid the ashtray next to the rose.

"Here, you put him out." Shai handed Pumfter to him, and Billy felt ashamed of the rage—Shai had been through the nightmare, too; he needed Pumfter just as much as Billy did.

Billy took a draft of Pumfter's friendly face in the moonlight. He remembered when Pumfter had been as big as another person in bed next to him. Although he hadn't kissed the dog for years, he knew exactly the feel of that felt nose, those rough seams. He didn't need to kiss him.

"All right," he said, and went up into the bushes and put Pumfter there. Then he huddled with Alex and Castle and Shai on the slope, watching Jo nervously.

"Go on, then, Jo," called Shai, then added very softly to the others, "Now think about that nice doggy."

Alex's free hand crept into Billy's. Billy went still, feeling grateful and responsible and unworthy.

And then the feelings squashed themselves, and their insides leaked everywhere. The sky opened up in a wide, tooth-edged smile, and a sour, loving fog filled the clearing. It thickened and warmed and became shaggy. Jo jumped about trying to grab handfuls of it; the others sank unconscious to the ground. The dog-ness nosed around them for a moment, nudged Billy, gave Jo's tiny hand a lick; then it sprang from the top of Cottinden's Hill and exploded into the wider world.

Corin broke gaze with Nance to look up. This third thing sopped up moon- and starlight as it came; it had a different darkness from the sky's—damp, gray-brown, ragged at its leading edge.

He half rose to meet it. The mist, which was the exact temperature of his own skin, took away his balance, lifted him off his feet. He tumbled, slowly, over and over, until he fetched up against some wall or planet. He sank away under the smell of dog fur and dog breath and wet, new grass, and was nowhere for a while.

The clink of flowerpot pieces brought him back, the breathing of that woman Rose, the paving under his hip, the wall under his boot; the fact that there was a house nearby and that it was their house, his and the woman Rose, the woman Nance's; the fact that every object in it, and in this garden, stood clean-edged, itself, and known to him.

They were walking along the path; they were helping each other along the path. They were very weak; they were a little hilarious with their weakness. Their legs were stumps and their arms were lumps and their heads were great heavy pots of brains, fitfully electric. Corin's ears seemed to be stuffed with cotton wool. The door—the thin slapping screen door that his hands knew every nail and board of, the screen with its summertime load of moths and lacewings—Rose opened it and admitted them to the house, and it felt like some sort of ceremony.

He was at the table trying to explain, talking loudly, clumsily through the cotton wool. *And being angry was a kind of paint,* he bellowed, *and I splashed it all over everything, and everything looked the same. Everything was just something that would make me angry again. Because-because-because-because. All those becauses, on and on—for years, Nance! For my whole life!*

Nance laughed and brought tea—in a cup!, gold-rimmed!, instead of his bitten-looking old mug that he might have insisted on. He rubbed the scarred table around the saucer wonderingly. *Do you think I've had some kind of stroke?*

*Well, if you have, we both have.* Her voice was woolly and distant. Her hair was bright white and wiry, and ashes and a leaf were caught in it. Her face was as old as his and laughing, and her eyes! My goodness, all their lives were in there. He would have to look more. He would have to ask her things—

And then, with a slap of door and a swirl of moths, here came the boy.

*Billy!* said Nance—even through the wool Corin heard how much was in her voice, was in the name. But by the fact that she left her body facing him as she turned to speak, he understood that she was sharing, not trying to claim the boy all to herself.

*You're asleep on your feet, my darling!* she said.

Billy stood the ashtray on the floor to free up a hand. He closed the door properly behind him. He came to the table and laid the rose there.

*I borrowed that*, he said, hugging the toy dog to his stomach. *It's still good. Maybe you can put it in one of those special vases, the ones for one flower.*

*A bud vase?* And Nance was up getting one.

Billy kept his gaze on the rose, and Corin looked him up and down. He felt he had never seen this boy before; he didn't know what to do with him besides beleaguer him.

He made his voice very low so that Billy would not mistake him. *How did the experiments go?*

Billy gave one eye a sketchy rub. *Well, he guessed everything.* His hair was dull with cobwebs and sweat.

*He's good, then?* Corin felt as if he were walking out onto water, using small steps, heel-to-toe, freezing the water with his feet as he went, to make something strong enough to walk on. *He's got the powers?*

Billy looked at him. Corin thought, *It's possible I've not met eyes with this boy before. And how old is he? Ten? Twelve? I should know what ten and twelve look like. I should know, from my own children.*

*He's got too much powers,* said Billy. *Says his mum, anyway; she says he's getting too good. She says him and Shai are like babies with a box of bombs. She's so angry. She's sending Jo to the You-Crane to learn from her uncle. That's a country.*

*The Ukraine? I've heard of it.*

Nance brought the rinsed bud vase to the table and put the rose in it.

*I really need a bath,* Billy said to her. Then he blinked. *So do you! And you too, Grandpa Corin. What've you been doing to get so dirty?*

They thought about that. Then Corin said gravely, *I put the bin out.*

Nance laughed. *Yes, and . . . and a bit of a wind came up.*

Billy looked from face to face. *I told Shai Cottinden's Hill wasn't far enough. Nowhere we could walk to would be.*

*You've been all the way to Cottinden's Hill?* Nance looked horrified.

*I know they felt it at Cowper Fen,* Billy said to Corin. *That's why their mum came and met us.*

*I think they might have felt it in the Ukraine,* said Corin. *I hope that uncle felt it, and comes running.* He finished his tea.

*Another?* said Nance.

*Yes, please.*

The empty cup gleamed in Corin's paw.

*I know that's fancier than you're used to,* Nance apologized, bringing the pot.

*It's good.* Corin clinked the cup onto its saucer. *It's fine.*

His ears popped and the cotton wool was gone from them. The tea clucked and pattered into the cup. "And then I'll get the bath on," said Nance. "But you'll want a smackle of something to eat, Billy. A round of sandwiches?"

"You go up," said Corin. "I can do that."

She looked at him doubtfully. But he knew if he let her feed the boy this time, tonight might as well not have happened.

"I'll make him one of my slabs," he said in the new low voice. "That'll fill him."

She smoothed her hair and went. He heard the sounds of Billy climbing into the chair right to the walls of the kitchen, and of Nance's feet on the stairs reverberating to the edges of the house, and beyond that was the garden and the summer night in all its size, with all its traffic of creatures and breezes and brooks and planetary light. And here he was in the middle of it, for the moment, in this house, in this room, moving from here to there gathering bread, gathering cheese and sausage and pickle, knife, board, plate—though he was not, himself, in any way, hungry at all.

# The Golden Shroud

I DISMOUNTED AS SOON AS I saw the round tower, its broken crenellations, its warning flag. I hobbled Goosestep and crept forward. The forest was harmless, sun-dappled, on all sides; birds fought and fluttered in their green houses, and sang soaring above them.

The witch's horse was not there. I broke from the trees, readying my throat to call.

But "Ah!" started from me, like a cry from the girl herself. The tower door was open. Light was piled golden before it, motionless fire, a weighty plaited sun.

My horror carried me to this wreckage, and buried my arms to the elbows in it. Was it still warm? Did she lie dead above? Did the witch await me?

Not caring—*daring* the witch, indeed, to present herself to me in my terror and rage—I ran in, I ran up. On a single breath, it felt, I reached the room.

The door stood wide. All was as it should be within, except that I entered this way, and into emptiness, not by the window and into my love's arms. How plain, how threadbare all this was without her, that had seemed such rich furnishings and so essential; how sad the little pillow on the bed where we had lain and whispered, how poor the rug, covering so few of the cold flags! And the chill! I had never felt it before. She and her hair had warmed this air before, her breath and life, the love we had built between us.

The mad fear seized me that as I gaped here, some animal, some thief, was carrying away that treasure below, and down I ran again. No, there it lay, all sumptuous as it had ever been.

I could not leave it, yet I could not carry such a weight—I had tried, marveling, laughing, often enough. She herself had kept it coiled on bed or wall, roaming from its weight only so far, like a tied dog. It was a cruelty to her, even as, pegged through on the sill, it had made our meeting possible; it had been my ladder to her and my line. *You can reel me in like a fish,* I had laughed to her. And unsmiling she replied, *Only if you are there below.*

I knelt and attacked the gold, unplaiting from the thick head-end, where the witch's sword or scissors had hacked. The stuff fell apart, slithered side to side, transformed, it seemed, into other matter: cascading water, rippling cloth-of-gold. Strands of it wandered in the air and at the edges. I fought it and wept; I was in a welter of goldness, up to my knees, bogged in beauty. Perhaps if I dug far enough I would find her, curled delicate as an ear underneath all this richness.

I did not, do I need say? The hair was spread, lacquering path and field like a syrup, materials for a thousand gorgeous bird nests, and she was gone. It was only as I loosed the ribbon at the narrower plait-end, and unworked the last several yards from there more easily, that cold realization came, and cooled my tears and my sweat, and sat in my heart like stone.

I lay in the slippery whorl of her hair, the spread sun on the ground, trailing and looping out into the green. I smelt, I felt, the grass through the perfumed strands pillowing my cheek. What had the old bitch done: Had she killed her? Had she worse? Had she found worse than this tower and this tether of hair?

I could not take all the hair, and I could not leave. I sat up and dashed the last cold tears from my eyes, and of the several strands caught in my fingers, I chose the strongest and brightest. Back through the labyrinth and tangle I followed it; I found one end, and from there looped it loose around three fingers, and wound it up, the full length, making a brighter and a solider ribbon, knuckle to knuckle, fattening, gleaming, scented with her loveliness.

When I had all of the strand, I bound it into itself and tucked it, narrow and bright as a bracelet made to the measure of her small wrist, into my belt satchel with all the gifts I had brought her: the foods from the palace, a piece of fine lace I had bought her at market, the jeweled comb.

"Well, this is pretty." The voice was cold and clear as October mornings.

I sprang to my feet. "I did not hear you."

"Ah, but I heard *you*."

Never had there been a crueler contrast than the sunlit spillage about my feet with the tall woman in the edge of the shadowed wood, white-faced above her black riding garb, her hand like a knot of bones in her stallion's reins, himself night-black and leering.

"I heard you long ago," she said, "when first you threatened to besmirch my lily. I heard you scrambling and your fondling fingers. I knew exactly, and from the beginning, what you sought. And that is all that matters: that you should not have it."

"Why not?" said I. "Why should I not have her, as my wedded wife? I am a prince, one day to be king of all lands east of here. Am I not man enough to husband her?"

She had been surveying the hair, but she looked up at me, and gave a faint snort. "That girl is part of such machinations, boy, your courtly politics are but a May dance, but a nodding daffy-dilly, beside them. Tut-tut! Such a mess you have made." She shook her head over the hair again. "It will be much less easy to bear away now."

In the instant I glanced down at the hair myself, she was dismounted and at me. In three strides only, she covered that impossible distance—I counted them even as they took no time at all. She pressed some rasping cloth or spell to my nose and mouth, that caught in my throat and closed it; she was muttering in my ear her witch language; she was strong, all iron and leather. But I barely had time to realize I could not fight her before I was gone insensible.

I woke immured in stone, behind an iron-barred door. I had been installed here who knew how long ago; who knew how long the witch's spell had lasted? All my limbs had forgotten themselves, so long had I lain. I could not tell how they were disposed. But as I woke, as I became myself again, a thread of voice sounded in my memory, a strand of sweetness, whispering: *Everything she says is some variety of lying. The trick*—I found my arms and pushed myself to sitting on the gritty flagstones—*the trick is to look to the side of what she says, and find the truth there.*

I was not in the round tower, but a larger place of stone. Poor light, inlet by not much more than arrow slits, showed me, beyond the door, a stairway leading up, turning a square corner and continuing. Was this the witch's castle? Did she prowl above? Or was this only the place she left her captives, to rot as they might, to scream at the deaf stone, the unheeding forest outside—or the sea, or the mountain steeps? Who could tell?

"Am I imprisoned alone?" I called, and no one answered. I crawled to the bars and knelt there listening, but there was no breath or cough or shifting of other persons. Silence poured thick into my ears, such nothingness as might still the very blood, if listened to for too long.

I pulled myself to standing; I was bruised but not in any way broken. I had been flung, perhaps, over her stallion's haunches, and carried sacklike some considerable way. For days, for months, who knew? Who knew I was not in some other time entirely, in some other enchanted place from which I might never return to my own palace, with its own cells that seemed from here such amiable places, the guards with their bowls and breads ambling about, some ne'er-do-well always protesting, or telling his adventure to his neighbor?

A stone shelf ran low along one side of my cell, that might be seat or bed or place of torture—old shackles lay there, open, chained to the wall stone. I went to it and experimented sitting; pains bloomed along my thighs and up my back, like lamps igniting blue and red. I drew my knees to my chest to explore the pains and stretch the muscles around them, maybe to ease them, and then I sat, a tiny cloud of breath and beating pulse in the lifelessness.

I still had my satchel at my belt; the witch had left me that, so little did she think of me. The comb inside was broken; the garnet once the center of a full-blown garnet rose tumbled loose in the satchel bottom, but this I thought was only from general rough treatment, not ill will of the witch. The food—that was what would be of use to me. I put aside the comb parts and the garnet, and the hair bracelet and the lace, which was now stained with the grease through the cured-salmon cloth, and I took out the foods that had only been for my love to taste and sample, not to sustain her—witch bread and witch meat did that. The fish was squashed but not spoiled; the cake was gone to crumbs in its cloth; the stone-fruits I had brought green so as to leave them with my love to ripen in my absence, and give her pleasure of me though I could not deliver it day by day, and they were still green, by magic or by lack of time.

I set myself to eating the cake, as the soonest-spoiling and the longest-eating. These were rich foods; I must eke them out, for who was to say that I was *not* in my own world, and missed from court, and parties sent out after me? It would not take Lewin Hawk long to track me to the tower, and thence to this place. I might be several days waiting, but all might not be lost, if Lewin brought a party of men against the witch.

The witch. The remains of her spell shuddered in my blood. *Ah, but I heard you.* I shook off the memory of her voice, her cold-white face. Death alone in prison I preferred to the thought of facing her again.

My fingers paused in their crumb gathering. They remembered—my whole hands remembered—holding the chopped end of my love's hair. A poor job the witch had made of it, all steps and jags and hackings. She had not snipped, composed, in cold revenge, but had gone at it in a rage, unthinking of the consequences in her surprise. She had not heard me at all—she had known nothing of me and suspected nothing. Whatever gift or keepsake she had found, whatever word my love had dropped, unwitting, that had betrayed us—that is what had precipitated that act of violence on the girl; there was no forethought in it at all. Everything the witch said—I put aside my cloth full of crumbs on the stone—was some sort of lie.

The hair bracelet glowed there, gathering and warming what

little light there was. I picked it up, and in doing so loosed the hair end I had tucked into the band after binding it. It sprang out and unwound three loops of the binding, with so much more energy than I would have credited the silky stuff that I gave it my full attention.

I held the bracelet flat on my palm. As if shyly now, the hair continued its unwinding twirl; then, when it apprehended that I was not afraid, with more confidence it drew itself away, freeing the loops entirely, and—this startled me a little, but with wonder rather than fear, and I had no wish for it to cease—shook itself into a loose spiral of moving gold. The end of it sat up like a serpent's head above its coil, seeming to regard me.

"Go on, then," I said, for the sight of this movement and life had warmed me to hope.

In answer, the hair strand made a most elegant leap from my palm. Its head stayed erect, but the coils fell to the filthy floor, and then the very tip flew at the lock of my prison door, and entered there the keyhole, taking after it a certain length of the gold. Within the chambers and workings it labored a while, until a muffled clank sounded and the door loosened in the frame. The hair passed out the other side of the lock, its closer end lashing to follow, bright as an arc of water caught by sunlight.

I upped and went after it, out of my jail room. The hair kept close to grounds and corners. If it had not clearly been my love's and my ally, I might have found quite sinister this line of light clinging and slithering ahead. Up the stairs we went, and around the square corner, and on. By the time I reached the upper door, the strand in its delicacy and enchantment had passed beyond it and lifted the weighty beam that made for a latch.

It led me through all the castle's ways. Quickly, but never too fast, it preceded me, soundless and shining along cold hall and dank corridor, doglegged up stair and down. At one place it leaped up, and noosed itself around my knees and drew me to the wall among the shadows while across the doorway ahead of us strode the tall, black-clad figure of the witch, her own iron-gray hair plaited in a crown about her head, her face coldly preoccupied. She walked on without hesitating, quite unaware of me and my guide. So much for her having felt my presence before.

We came to a tower door, which the golden strand negotiated with the same strength and intelligence as it had overcome other obstacles. Firmly it closed and locked the door behind us—I heard its smooth machinations within the lock as I waited on the darkened steps—and then by its faint light I walked up and around a dizzying long way, its golden zigzag fast to the wall corner beside my climbing feet.

We passed several doors, but the one where the hair strand broke from its zigzagging and leaped to the lock had life behind it, in the form of my love's weeping. I pressed my hands against the wood as the magic worked in the lock, and then the door gave and there I was, released into a room even dimmer and narrower and poorer furnished than had housed her before, with my poor shorn girl a-weeping on no more than a lumpy palliasse, and none too fresh-looking at that, along one wall.

"Come now," I said, kneeling by her. "Come, come. What can tears achieve, my dearest?"

I only glimpsed her tear-aglow face for a moment. Unburdened by her great hair, she flung herself up to me, weeping afresh and exclaiming into my neck. I lifted her—I *could* lift her now, without that rope restraining her to the ground—and carried her lightness to the arrow-slit window, and held her there for several moments of glorying, in my freedom from the witch's penning below, in the sweetness and slenderness and live weeping warmth of my love's embrace.

"We must away, though," I said to her eventually.

"Away?" she said. "But how? How indeed came you here? Followed us on Goosestep? Oh, but I looked for you as we rode away—until she slapped me and told me keep my face forward."

"By spell and by sorcery I came," I said. "And not all that witch's. We have a friend, my sweet. We have many friends in this castle, many strands of friends."

She watched me smile, wiping tear stripes from her lovely cheek. That friend of mine, I saw, had come to her unnoticed, and lay loose around her neck, drops of salt sorrow in its strands here and there like smooth-tumbled crystals in a cunning necklace.

I kissed her and stood her on her feet, and took her slim hand. Her freed hair sprang and swung in curls about her head and shoulders, lovelier than ever.

"Let us go," I said.

"She will prevent us, surely?" But she followed me out the door and down the stair.

"She will try, I am sure."

I led my lady down, into the body of the castle. Now I knew my own way, and I took us to the place where I had last seen the witch.

Gently I covered my love's mouth and whispered to her necklet: "Go, friend: find the witch and assemble your sisters against her."

"Hush," I told my love's terror, and I held her hands down as the hair strand unwhipped from around her neck and snaked away.

"But what—?"

"Follow," I said, and took her hand, and we ran swiftly and silently after the swift silent streak of magic that lately had been part of her.

It ran too swiftly for us in the end, out of our sight, but that hardly mattered, for "What?" and "No!" the witch cried distantly, and then "No, never!" and then her screams, enraged beyond words and then fearful, then desperate from her struggles, led us on.

A golden light played against the wall, opposite the room she fought in. I stepped into that light, and drew my love after me into it, and held her to me with both arms, that she should see her tormenter overcome.

The room was a storm of golden hair. Through the beat

and fog of it I saw the wooden beams of the witch's loom, on which she had been winding my love's hair as warp, and from which those threads now flailed and loosened. For the rest, for the hairs that had lain about the room in withy baskets, they were up and about the woman, and those that could not reach her flew and fretted in the airs around as their sisters bound the old horror in a golden shroud, as they masked her bony face and gaping mouth in shining gold, as they spun and cabled themselves and noosed her evil neck, and tightened, tightening her to silence, trapping the dead breath inside her and shutting the live air out. And the tighter they grew, the limper and quieter fell the witch, until she was nothing but a golden rag, laid to the flags on strands flung down like rushes, and rained upon, snowed upon, covered and blurred by falling strands of my love's hair, swaths of the golden magic, of the power we had made together out of nothing more than our affections and our selves.

We rode home together, my love astride Goosestep, myself on the leery black, tamed by a harness of hair. We had buried the witch behind us, with stones on her head and heart and a golden net about her to keep her in the ground forever. Several strands we had kept aside, for the purposes of leading us to my father's castle from this outland, and keeping us from danger along the way. The remainder of the hair had plaited and put itself away in the baskets, and these our horses bore as panniers.

## The Golden Shroud

Side by side we traveled, and if the forest ways grew narrow I fell back, so that my love should have the assurance of her sisters running ahead and her betrothed riding behind as she went through strange country toward her new home, the hair that was left to her light upon her shoulders, soft beside her sun-kissed cheeks, and borne up and flying like so many guardian birds or butterflies, on any breeze happening by.

# A Fine Magic

Well, in the town where these two beautiful daughters lived there was a fascinator, name of Gallantine. He was neither young nor handsome, but he had no wife and he was as interested as any of the young men were in getting one of the girls—if not the rich elder girl, the more beautiful younger one. Whichever he won, he would be an object of other men's envy—and even magic men are not immune to wanting that.

Gallantine did all the things that those young men were trying. First he put himself regularly in the young women's way, happening by outside their house just as they crossed from door to carriage, or arriving at the edge of the path as they made their daily park promenade. Tall and thin in his dark suit, he lifted his dark hat and lowered his gaze to their lovely feet as they passed.

On one of these occasions, seeing that the mamma's carry

dog was suffering some kind of skin affliction, he struck up a conversation with her, professing more interest than he truly felt in the care of such animals. Afterward he sent her a pot of a cream to apply to the dog's skin. He had magicked the cream both to cure the lesions and to engender tenderness toward himself in any person who touched it. Which ended with my lady's chambermaid developing quite a crush on him, while Mamma herself, who almost always wore gloves when carrying the dog, came no closer than being able to abide having Gallantine near, where before she had felt a natural repugnance toward his self-conscious bearing, his funereal clothes and his conspicuous lack of associates or friends. The two beautiful daughters, who thoroughly disliked the dog, no more noticed him than they noticed iron fence posts or singular grass blades among the many.

Gallantine was thus driven to exert his powers more forcefully to impress himself upon the young ladies. By various subtle hand wavings he managed to obtain an invitation to one of the mamma's afternoons, and to hold the girls' admirers at bay long enough to engage first the older, then the younger, in several minutes' "conversation," during which each responded most politely to his observations on the weather, the present company and the pleasantness of walking in parks.

He came away satisfied that he had fixed himself in their memories as an intriguing man of the world. He read interest into the smiles he had collected, quickenings of the heart into the girls' casting their glances downward or away from him. He was very hopeful of his chances with either of the lovelies.

He next engineered his attendance at a ball at which the daughters were to be present. He went to great pains and some expense to prepare himself, traveling up to the port city to have himself outfitted by a good tailor. Once he was dressed, he put what he felt must be an irresistible glamour all around himself, and he was rewarded at the ball by many glances, dances and fan-flutterings from the older women, as well as a dance with each of the daughters. He was light on his feet, you can imagine, which left the girls free to concentrate on words, and words they had in plenty, buoyed up by their excitement at being out in society and by far the most marriageable persons in the room, indeed in the town. Gallantine read their happy chatter entirely as regard for himself. Watching them in exactly the same play with others on the dance floor, he thought the girls very kind for their patience with lesser men when their hearts were so clearly leaning and yearning toward his own.

When he felt that enough such meetings had taken place, Gallantine made his feelings known, first to the older daughter and then, on being rejected by her repeatedly, to the younger. At first made gentle by her own surprise and by the strong glamours he had carried to the meeting, this lovely girl did not utterly reject him, but soon, with her sister's and her mother's horrified exclamations ringing in her ears, she found sufficient will, reinforced by true and natural feelings of revulsion, to be definite enough in her refusal of him that he could hold no further hopes of a match with her.

Well, it's never a good idea to get on the wrong side of

a fascinator, is it? For he's unlikely just to retire and lick his wounds. Gallantine went off to his house—which was not small and not large, and not in a good part of town nor yet in a bad, but which of course bore no womanly touches barring some lace at the windows put there by his late mother that, if touched (which it never was), would have crumbled from age and poor quality—and he brewed himself a fine magic. It was so powerful that to all intents and purposes Gallantine did not exist for a while, except as instrument or agent of his own urge to revenge. And so at this point in the story it behooves us to leave Gallantine in his formless obsession and join the two daughters, through whose eyes the working-out of that obsession is much clearer.

So here is the younger girl, alone in her room, sitting up in bed writing a breathless account of that evening's events in her day journal.

And here is the older, sitting more solemnly in front of her mirror, having just accepted (her father is to be consulted tomorrow) an offer of marriage from a most suitable gentleman: young, fine-looking and possessed of a solid fortune, and of a character to which her heart can genuinely warm.

Under each girl's door, with a small but significant sound, is slipped a white envelope. Each starts up, and crosses her room; each takes the envelope up and listens for—but does not hear—receding footsteps outside. The seal on the envelope is unfamiliar, marvelous; breaking it releases a clean, piney, adventurous scent onto the bedroom air, and each girl breathes this scent in.

# A Fine Magic

*Step through the door,* says the card inside. Each girl hesitates, then reaches to take the doorknob. But the doorknob won't be taken, will it? The hands—the younger tentative, the older more resolute—close to fists on nothing.

*Step through the door.* Two hands touch two doors, and find the timber to be, in fact, a stable brown smoke. The hands sink into the surface; the smoke curls above the pale skin like stirred-up silt. The moment passes when they might choose whether to stay or go, and they step through.

And they are in a wood, a dim, cold, motionless wood. The trees are poles of indigo with maybe foliage, maybe cloud, on high. The light is blue; the ground is covered with drifts of snow.

They see each other, the one in her white nightgown and wrap, the other in her dance dress, the hothouse orchid still in her hair. Each gives a cry of relief, and they run together.

"I'm so glad you're here, sister!"

"Where are we? In a dream?"

"I've never known a dream so cold!"

They clutch arms and look around.

"There, look! Is that a fire?" For warm yellow lights move, far off among the trees.

"It must be! Let us go and warm ourselves!"

They set off. Bare or in thin embroidered slippers, their feet are soon numb with cold. But the ground under the snow is even, and the strange trees are smooth and sprout no projections to catch their clothing or otherwise hinder them. Music floats to meet them, music such as they've never danced to, beguiling, rhythmical, minor-keyed. Their minds don't know what to make of it. It seems ugly, yet it attracts them. It is clumsily, grossly appropriate. It is a puzzle, and to solve it they must move closer and hear it more clearly.

Apart from this music the wood is like a large and silent room. No bird flies through it; no wind disturbs the air. The chill rises like a blue fume from the snow; it showers with the gray light from above.

The music deepens and brightens as they stumble on; various hummings as of rubbed wet crystal, and many different pitches of tinkling, or jingling, adorn its upper reaches. It grows other sounds that are nearly voices, uttering nearly words, words the two daughters want to hear, are convinced they must hear, if they are to understand this adventure. A deep, slow, sliding groan travels to them through the ground.

"It is!" says the older girl, peering around a tree. "It's a carousel! An enormous one! Beautiful!"

"Oh, I'm so cold!"

They hurry now, and soon are in the clearing where the magnificent creation revolves. The music is rosy-fleshed arms gathering them up in a dance; the horses rise and fall with the rhythm, the foxes, too, the carriages and sleighs, the swans and cats and elephants. The lightbulbs are golden; the mirrors shed sunlight, the carven faces laughter; the revolving makes a breeze that flows warmly springlike out into the daughters' faces, that lifts the manes and tails and furs and feathers of the carved animals, that brightens the horses' flanks until the older girl is convinced she sees galloping muscles move, until the younger would vow on a Bible that she saw a fly land on that bay's shoulder, and be shaken off by a flesh tremor.

And they would swear that, for a moment, the creatures and sleighs carried figures: pretty girls in their detailed fashions, fine-figured young men waving their hats, all with such joyful expressions, all with such eagerness in their bodies and gestures, that the daughters' single impulse is to join them, to be in among the throng, so warm in color and mood, to be swept up and a part of that strange heavy-lively crystalline music—

Which winds up, with a spirited suddenness, to a triumphant flourish, and stops. There is no one on the carousel. Only the creatures stand in the golden light, a hoof raised here, a head lowered there. Then the hoof strikes the wooden floor, the head lifts and the lips whiffle; an ostrich turns and blinks at the daughters down its beak. Life, minor life, entrances each girl's eye.

"Look, the eagle! His wings are like fire!"

"So beautiful! So warm! I wish that music would start again."

They stand in the snow, clutching each other.

"Do you suppose we are meant to ride it? In this dream?"

"Look, there are steps up to it—of course we are, sister! Come! Which mount will you choose?"

"Oh, are you sure?" But she climbs the stairs after her sister.

And there follows delight—the last delight of their lives. They run about, in the warmth, with no mammas or chaperones to restrain them, choosing now the lion for his sumptuous warm mane and wise eye; now the cat for its flexibility and fur and for the fish, flashing rainbows, it holds in its jaws; now the sleigh for its quilts and candles; now the eagle again for the grandeur of his red-gold wings.

Finally, the elder daughter chooses the black stallion with the bejeweled harness and the saddle of warm bronze leather. The younger finds a strawberry roan nearby with an improbably frothing cream mane, all its harness a supple blood-red. She climbs astride and it tosses its head, showering her with tiny white blossoms, sweetly scented, that melt like snowflakes on her skin. Delighted, she turns to her sister, in time to see her glister with tiny melting gems, shaken from the coal-black's mane.

"What bewitching animals!" she cries—then "Oh!" as the beautiful machine creeps into motion around them. The music bursts out from the central fantasia of mirrors and organ pipes and glossy-colored figures and gold-painted arabesques.

All is beautiful and wonderful, warm and alive, while the carousel gathers speed. Everywhere they look something catches the eye: the deft paintwork that makes that cherub look so cunning; the glitter of eagle feathers as the lights pass over; the way the giraffe runs beside them, clumsy and elegant at the same time; the lozenges of *trompe l'œil* that offer whole worlds in a glance, brine-plashy seascapes, folly-bedecked parks, city squares thronged with characters and statuary, alpine vistas where one might as easily spring up into the sky as tumble to the crags below.

And their ears and their hearts are too full of the weighty

rhythms of the music to allow proper thought. And the beasts below them are just alive enough to intrigue them, and to respond to the supple reins. The carousel reaches its full speed, and they gallop there awhile, calling to each other, perfectly happy.

And then it spins just a little faster.

The music accelerates, veers upward in pitch, sounds a little mad, a little wild. There is a jerk as of slipping gear wheels, and the roan plunges.

"Sister!" The younger girl grasps the gold-and-white-striped pole to which the horse is fixed.

But her sister is wrestling with the reins of her own bounding stallion. Now, half-tossed from the saddle, she clings to the horse's pole, struggles to regain her seat.

So frightened are they, so dizzied by the machine's whirling, so busy with their desperate cries for each other's aid, that they do not see the shiny paintwork of the poles fade to a glassy blue in their grasp, the warmer colors drain down, down out of the poles entirely. They do not discover until too late that—

"Sister, my hands! They are frozen fast!"

The machine and the music spin on, but the horses' movements slow and cease. Their painted coats—glossy black, pink-brown—fade to blue where the pole strikes through them, and the blueness spreads across the saddles under the folds of nightgown and dance dress. The girls' fine cotton drawers are no protection against the terrible coldness. It locks their thighs to the saddles; it locks their seats; it strikes up into their women's parts, fast as flame, clear as glass, cold as ice.

"Sister!"

"Sister, help me!"

They gaze aghast at each other. The animals between and around them fade to blue, freeze to stillness, beaks agape, teeth points of icy light, manes and tails carven ice. The music raves, high-pitched and hurrying. The golden lights become ice bulbs gathering only the blue snow-light below, the gray cloud-light above. The forest spins around the carousel, a mad, icy blur.

The park promenade. It is early spring and still quite cold.

Gallantine, raising his hat to every muffled personage who passes, is older now; his figure is fuller, almost imposing in the well-cut dark coat. His new wife, upon his arm, is slender, dark-haired, and has more than a touch of magic about her.

She glances over her shoulder, back along the path. "If I'm not mistaken," she says, removing her hand from his arm and placing it in her ermine muff, "one of those ladies once had a place in your affections."

"The Leblanc sisters? Well, they were beauties in their time, though you may find that hard to credit now."

"Did they always clutch each other so?" she says, glancing back again. "Did they always carry themselves in that strange way?"

"On the contrary, they were very fine dancers, once," says Gallantine mildly.

His wife is silent until he will look at her, and then for a while of looking.

She laughs a very little, through her beautiful nose. "How very gauche," she murmurs, narrowing her eyes at him. "How very crude of you." Her mouth is lovely, too. It is the only spot of color in the whole wintry park. She hisses at him, almost inaudibly. "There are so many things for which to *punish* you."

"Madam." His voice cracks with gratification. He offers her his arm.

She reattaches herself to him, and they walk on.

# An Honest Day's Work

Jupi's talkie-walkie crackled beside his plate. Someone jabbered out of it, "You about, chief?"

All four of us stopped chewing. We'd been eating slowly, silently. We all knew that this was nearly the last of our peasepaste and drum bread.

Jupi raised his eyebrows and finished his mouthful. "Harrump." He brushed the flour from the drum bread off his fingers. He picked up the talkie and took it out into the courtyard. Jumi watched him go, eyes glittering, hands joined and pointing to her chin.

"Couldn't have come at a better time," said Dochi. "Eat something other than pease for a change." He rolled his eyes at me.

"Eh. Pease is better than nothing, like some people have," I said, but mildly. You don't pick a fight with the prince of the household.

"Shh!" said Jumi, leaning toward the courtyard door.

"Why don't you go out?" Dochi pushed his face at her. "Listen right up close?" Dochi was sound in body, so could get away with rudeness. With my withered leg I had to be more careful.

"Shh!" she said again, and we listened.

From the squeal of the voice and the way it worried on and on, it was Mavourn on the other end—and from Jupi's barking answers: "Yup . . . I'll be there. . . . I'll fetch him on the way. . . . Yup." Behind his voice blue-daubs buzzed in the neighbor's bananas, tearing strings off the leaves for nesting. Farther away were the cries of sea birds, and of that family down the lane that always fought, that no one spoke the names of.

Then Jupi was in the doorway, the talkie clapped closed in his hand, his arms spread as if to receive, as only his due, this gift from heaven.

Jumi smiled frightenedly. "Incoming?" she said.

Jupi tipped his head.

"A big one?"

"Mavourn says one leg and one arm, but sizeable. Good big head, good sex. Not junk, he says."

Jumi clapped her hands, sparkling. Then she went modest, pulled the cloth farther forward around her face, and ushered our emptied plates toward herself. The anxiety was gone that had been tightening her like slow-wrung laundry these past weeks.

And for us, too, all of a sudden the evening's heat and approaching darkness weren't oppressive anymore. We didn't need to flee from worried thoughts into sleep.

"So I can be useful, too?" I said. "If it's sizeable?"

Dochi snorted, but Jupi blessed me with a nod. "Amarlis can have work, too, as I arranged with A. M. Agency Limited. Just as I arranged it, it comes to be, does it not?"

Jumi pushed the pease bowl and the bread platter toward him. "Eat," she said. "You will need your strength for working."

So we went to the office of A. M. Agency Limited, and saw their hiring officer, and I was taken on as a team onlooker, and put my mark on the dotted line.

"Well, there is no problem with the boy's hand, at least," said the hirer's assistant. He thought it was a kind of joke.

Jupi could have said, *Oh no, he makes a good mark.* Or *That's right, every other part of him is fine and sound.* Or *There are many activities for which two good legs are not needed.* Instead, he went icy quiet beside me.

I didn't mind what the man said. I was too happy to mind. I had a contract and I was going to do a useful job like any man— why would I care what anyone said? It was a nuisance only because Jupi minded so much that I had to mind on *his* behalf. And because, when we had finished our business, I had to swing along so fast and chatter so hard to make Jupi give up his minding with a laugh and hurry after me, and answer my questions.

Next morning before dawn we took my job ticket to the Commstore, and in the middle of the wonderful bustle there I was issued my onlooker's whistle and megaphone. Jumi had plaited me a neck cord for the megaphone that would hold it close on my back while I walked so I could manage the crutches, and loose at my hip when I stood at my work and might need to reach for it fast.

Then we went down to number 17 *plan* to await the incoming.

The boss men and the gangers grouped themselves, tense and sober, around my jupi and his crackling talkie. My brother Dochi and his friends formed another group, as they did outside The Lips Club most nights, only without the showy bursts of laughter. They were tired; they were missing their sleep-in.

I was in the main crowd of workers. As soon as the general shape and proportions of the incoming were clear, we'd be teamed up. There was not much talk, just watching the bay and shivering in the breeze. Many of us wore the new Commstore shirts, bought on credit when the news came yesterday. The dull pink and mauve stripes were invisible in the dusky light, but the hot green-blue stripes glowed, slashing down a man's left chest, maybe, with another spot on his right collar. To my eyes, as I read the *plan* over and over, trying to make it real, trying to believe my luck, the crowd was sticks and spots floating in darkness, with a movement to it like long grass in a slow wind.

Every now and then another team onlooker would come clearer against the others, his whistle a gleam, his megaphone swinging in his hand. These men I examined keenly; I was one of them now. I thought they all looked very professional. Their heads must be full of all manner of lore and experience, I was sure, and my own memory seemed very empty by comparison. Home life at my jumi's side was all I knew; I felt as if I ought to be ashamed of it, even as a pang of missing-Jumi made me move uncomfortably on the *plan*'s damp concrete.

*Won't this house be quiet without my little monkey!* she had said this morning.

Which had made me feel peculiar—guilty because I'd not even thought about how Jumi might feel, that I was going to work; flustered and a little angry, it must be confessed, because it seemed that I could do no right, I could be a sort of stay-at-home embarrassing half-person by her side, or I could be a cruel son leaving her lonely.

While I was feeling all this, Dochi gave one of his awful laughs. *Yes, he's such a screecher of a monkey,* he said. *So loud as he swings from tree to tree!*

Jumi gave him her mildest reproving look. She broke the soft-boiled egg and laid it on top of my soup in the bowl and pushed it toward me, under Dochi's laughing at his own joke, which she was not making him stop.

# Yellowcake

*Thank you, Jumi,* I said.

The joke was that I was so quiet and so little trouble, anyone could ignore me if they chose. The joke was that, after some years of trying, of lashing out at Dochi with my crutches and being beaten for it, I would rather sit as I did now at my food, wearing a blank look, and let the laughter pass by.

The incoming appeared on the horizon like a small, weak sunrise. The workers stirred and gestured, and another layer bobbed above the shirt stripes, of smiling teeth, of wide, bright eyes. My jupi barked into the talkie, and the two tugboats crawled out from the headland's shadow. They sent back on the breeze a whiff of diesel, and many noses drew it in with delight—a breakyard is *supposed* to be all smells and activity. How long had it been since Portellian smelt right and busy? Long enough for all our savings to be spent. Long enough for us to be half a sack of pease, quarter a sack of drum flour away from starting starving.

At first, all we could see was the backlit bulk of the thing, with a few bright rags of aura streaming in the wind, thinning as it came closer. The light from the sun, which as yet was below the horizon, made the thick shroud glow, and the body shape was a dark blur within it. I thought I could see a head, against a bigger torso. But you can't be sure with these things; they're never the same twice in their build and features, in their arrangement of limbs.

What kind of people could afford to send craft up into the ether to find and kill such beasts? They must be so rich! A boy

66

born bung-legged to those people would be no shame or disadvantage, I was sure—they would get him a new leg and sew that on. Or they would get him a little car, to drive himself around on their smooth roads. There would be so many jobs for him, his leg wouldn't matter; he might do finecrafts with his hands, or grow a famous brain, or work with computers. Nobody would be anxious for him or disappointed; he wouldn't have to forever apologize for himself and make up to his family for having come out wrong.

"It's a long-hair, I think," said someone near me. "I think I can see hair around that head—if it *is* the head."

"Hair? That's good."

"Oh, every part of it is good."

"It's low in the water," said another. "Good and fresh. Quality cuttings. Everything cheaper to process. Bosses will be happy."

"Everyone will be happy!"

People laughed. Now we could see that the thing was more than rumor and hope.

"I will be happy when I hold that new reel of net yarn in my hands."

"I will be happy when I'm seated in the Club with the biggest plate of char fish and onion in front of me—"

"And Cacohao, he'll be happy when he's lying in the dirt *behind* the Club—won't you, Caco?—singing love songs to a bottle of best throb-head."

"Oh. I can see her beautiful face now!"

People were spending their day wage all around me. But

when the incoming reached the tugs, and they attached their ropes and lined it up for the tide to bring it onto number 17, all fell quiet. The beast's head loomed, a soft dark shape inside the radiant shroud, which had protected the skin from damage during the burning of the aura. The shape beyond the head was long, narrow, uneven, with a lump at the foot. Jupi jabbered nervously on the talkie to the tugs, checked the time on the clock tower, and his gang around him grew now murmurous with advice, now silent with attention. Things could go wrong at this point; the moment must be judged exactly.

A breeze came ahead of the beast. Our shirts rattled on us; the hems of pants and loongies stung our calves. The air stank of the burnt plastics of the aura, a terrible smell that all the children of Portellian learned early to love, because it meant full bellies, smiling jupis and jumis. Coming in from the ether burnt the aura to almost nothing, to the pale dust we'd seen on the wind (all gone now), to this nasty smell. The sun crept up and took a chink out of the horizon. A lot of the men had gone forward into the mauve and silver wavelets that crawled up the *plan*.

The tugs, now unhooked from the beast, rode beside it, their engines laboring against the tide. Jupi stood with his arms folded, chewing his lip with the responsibility. The tugs retreated to the beast's far end, and with Jupi warning and checking them through the talkie, helped the tide move the great shape the last little way to the *plan*. The head began to rise independently of the body, nudged upward by the *plan*'s slope. A cheer went up; the beast was arrived.

Teams were forming. Horse piecers gathered with their spades at the head of the *plan* near the winches. Mincers, some with their own knives, drifted toward the try house, where the copper pots and boilers glowed in the shadows. Gangers came through the crowd shouting, claiming the workers they knew were good. As a team onlooker, I didn't have to jump and wave my arms and call out gangers' names. I was a contractor, not a loose day-job man dependent on luck and favor. I could stand calm in the middle of the scramble.

As the incoming edged up the *plan*, the cutting teams threw grapplers and swung themselves up the cloudy gel. Though they mustn't drop any gel while the beast was moving, they could make all their preparatory slits. This they did with ropes and weights, pulling the ropes through the gel just the way a merchant cuts wax-cheese with a wire. The shroud began to look fringed about the head and shoulders. The nimble rope-clippers darted in and out; chanters' voices rang on the stinking air from high on the beast's torso.

The message came through on the talkie: the tugs were done. The beast was beached, all head to foot of it. Jupi walked up the *plan* and signaled the bellman. The bell clanged, the teams cheered, the ground teams scuttled away from the body. Great strips of the gel began tumbling from above. They splashed in the shallows and bounced and jounced and sometimes leaped into curls across the other strips. Hookmen straightened them flat on the ground, making a wide platform on which the beast's parts could be deposited.

Another smell took over from the burnt-shroud odor. I had smelt it before as I helped Jumi, as I cleaned and cooked and span. She would lift her head, happy because the work—Jupi's and Dochi's work—was going on, and if one of the other mothers was there, she would say, *Smell that? It always reminds me of the smell of Dochi when he was born. Like inside-of-body, but clean, clean. New.*

*Smell of clean, warm womb,* the other might say.

*Yes, and hot, too! Hot from me and hot from him.*

When I was born to her, I must have smelt not so good, not so enchanting, for it was always Dochi she mentioned. Maybe it was only the firstborn who brought out the clean smell with him. I did not want the details of in what way I had smelt bad—or perhaps, how she had not noticed my smell from being in such horror at my leg. So I never asked.

Anyway, there would be other smells soon against this one: oil and fuel, sweat and scorched rope, hot metal, sawn bone, sea and mud and stirred-up putrefaction.

"Amarlis?"

The way I sprang to face Mavourn showed that I'd been waiting not moments but *years* to hear my name, to be called to usefulness.

"I'm putting you on a thigh team," he said. "It's got a good man, Mister Chopes, heading it. Are you happy with that?"

"Very happy, sir!"

"There is Mister Chopes with the kerchief on his head. I've told him you're on your way."

"And I am!"

I swung myself across the watery *plan*, watching Mister Chopes count heads, scan the hopping hopefuls, pick out a good clean man and give him a job ticket, shoo away a sneaky-looking boy. The team's chanter stood with his drum and beaters, wrapped in his white cloth and his dignity. He too was a contractor; he had no need to fuss.

Mister Chopes counted again, then sent them off for their hooks and spades, and turned and saw me. "You Amarlis?"

"I am, sir, Mister Chopes!"

"You ready to look sharp?"

"Sharp as a shark tooth, sir!"

"Mavourn says you'll be good, but you're new, right?"

"That's right, sir. This is my first day ever."

"I'll give you plenty of advice, then. You won't sulk at that, boy? You'll take that in good spirit?"

"I'll be grateful for all you can give me."

"Then we'll do fine. Main thing, no one gets hurt. All those boys have mothers. All those men have wives and children waiting on them, right? Your job's to make sure they come home on their own legs, right? Not flat and busted by beast bits. This here is Trawbrij; he's our chanter."

"How do you do, Trawbrij?" I shook hands with him.

"Twenty years on the *plans*," said Mister Chopes. "He'll tell

71

you anything more you need to know. Now, let's get down the thigh." Because all the team was tooled up and running back to us.

Some of the hopefuls, lingering nearby in case Mister Chopes changed his mind, cast jealous looks at me. They were angry, no doubt, that someone so clearly handicapped could gain a job when they, able-bodied, could not. I swung away from them.

Trawbrij the chanter gave us a beat; I walked with him, behind the twenty-five chosen workers, while Mister Chopes went ahead. The knee team preceded us, with their chanter and their onlooker; I tried to hold my head as high and my back as straight as their onlooker's, to look as casual and unself-conscious as he.

We took a safe path wide of the torso, well behind the row of waiting hookmen. Slabs of shroud slapped down and jiggled on the *plan*, sending wavelets over the hookmen's feet.

I had watched other incomings, up with the women and children on the hill behind town. What you don't see from there are the surfaces of things: the coarse head-hair, which is like a great tangle of endless, curving double-edged combs; the damp, waxy skin, pale as the moon, hazed with its own form of hair, dewy with packaging fluid; the eye, the ear hole and the mouth slit, all sealed with gray gum by the hunters. What you don't see from the hills is the *size*, is the *wall* of the cheek going up, behind the heaps of the hair, which themselves tower three houses high above the running workers. My eyes couldn't believe what was in front of them.

"He's enormous, isn't he?" said Trawbrij beside me.

"He makes us look like ants," I said. "Smaller than ants, even. Just look how much of the sky he takes up!"

"And yet we smaller-than-ants, we little crawling germs, we're going to set upon him, and pull him apart and bring him down and saw him into plates, and melt him into pots and pints, and there'll be nothing left of him in three weeks' time."

"Is there any part of him that's not useful to someone?" I turned to look properly at the chanter. He was slender and white-haired and wise-looking.

"I have only ever seen tumor rocks left lying on the *plan*, though even these reduce in time, and become parts of people's walls and houses, though they do not export. And sometimes if an organ bursts, or if the tides delay the incoming and the beast is putrefying on arrival, there may be lumps of dirty gel that won't melt, that sit about for a while."

As we came level with the thigh, the first of our team threw up his grappler and shinnied up the rope, chopping footholds as he went. Others followed, each just far enough behind the previous man not to be kicked in the head. In this way we quickly had half a team at the top.

Mister Chopes turned with his foot in the first slot. "Where's my looker? Amarlis."

"Here," I said.

"What do you reckon your job is?"

"Keep an eye out down here."

" 'S right. Main thing is, teams getting in each other's ways.

So, stand well back, watch how stuff falls and give a hoy before someone gets hurt."

"I'm on it."

I swung around, passed Trawbrij tucking up his robes for the climb and went back as far as the other onlookers. There I could see right to the edges of my team's activities, and keep track of Mister Chopes and the team up on top. I blew my whistle straightaway, and the whole ground team turned as if I had them on strings.

I cleared my throat. "Back up," I said clearly through the megaphone, and waved them toward me. "Back to where these other teams are standing." And up they came to safety, which seemed a wonder to me, a great respectful gesture. I tried not to smile, not to look surprised.

The shroud on the side of the thigh, because it was so flat, could be cut away in a single piece. When it came down—with a smack and two bounces that I felt up my spine and in my arm-pits through the crutches—there above it was the white-clay wall of the thigh, height of a tanker ship, running with pack fluid. That clean, warm, newborn-Dochi smell was all there was to breathe now. The fluid ran off, and the skin-hairs lifted from the skin, then separated from each other, gleaming in the early sun. And as I watched, the side-lit skin covered itself with little bluish triangles, bluish scallops of shadow, as if the hairs were not just drying and springing free but pulling bumps up on the skin, in the sudden chill of the sea breeze.

But then, without warning, the whole leg sprang free of the *plan*. Daylight shone underneath it, and watersplash, and I saw the tiny black feet of the far thigh team fleeing—and in my fright I forgot about the gooseflesh on the thigh.

The limb smacked back down, and did not move again.

One man on my team had been shaken loose. He hung swinging and screaming from the cutting-rope. Several farther down the limb had fallen right off the top. Some had hit the gel; two had bounced from it onto the *plan*. Out of all the sounds that happened in those few moments, I managed to hear the ones their heads made breaking on the ground two teams away. It sounded unremarkable, like wooden mallets striking the concrete, but of course they were not tools but people who struck, not wood but brother or father or son, as Mister Chopes had said. My heart rushed out—but less to the fallen ones than to their onlooker. He could have done nothing, poor man, it had happened so quickly. How anguished he must be! What a failure I would feel, if that were me! And then relief swept through me, a professional relief, that it had *not* been me, here on my first day.

All our team, except for those helping the hanging worker, were clawing gel, or each other, or watery ground, trying to hold the world steady. "How can such a thing happen?" I said to the man nearest me.

"It's a nerve thing," he said. "I've heard of it. It's electricity. It's metal on a nerve. It'll be that team on the knee. See how they've just shot their cap lever in there? You can do the same thing to a dead frog. Poke it in the nerve and the leg jumps, though the heart is still and the head is cut right off."

"Don't the bosses know about that nerve?" I said. "Shouldn't they have the knee team do their work first, rather than endanger so many workers?"

The man shrugged. "When no two beasts are quite the same, how is anyone to learn all the nerves?"

A boss and some stretcher men had run past us toward the shin, followed by day jobbers eager to offer themselves as replacements for the dead and the injured. Mister Chopes got his top team up and moving again. The hip men were back at work; the knee people cleavered open flesh so that the kneecap could be brought free; the wall of the thigh was smooth, sunlit. The hairs had a slight red-gold tint; perhaps that was why the flesh looked so rosy in the strengthening sun.

Once all the shroud was off the thigh, our job was a plain job, a meat job. The top team cut blanket pieces of thigh flesh and lowered them to the ground team. Hooked ropes were brought along from the winches at the top of the *plan,* and the ground team hooked the flesh on, then jumped aside as it slid away, followed by the flesh from the calf cutters, smaller and more shaped pieces than ours.

The hip team to our left didn't send anything up on the first load rope, or the second. Theirs was more technical work, cutting away the bags and scrags that were the beast's sex, sewing and sealing up the bags and passing them down in tarpaulin sheathing so that not a drop of the profitable aphrodisiacs could seep out and be wasted on the *plan*, on our splashing feet, on the sea. Then they must excavate the pelvis, which was complicated—valuable organs lay there and must not be punctured in the processing.

"That's a lot of muck, on the shroud," someone said as the smallest of the three toes, on the last few rope hooks, slid up past us.

" 'Cause it's so fresh," came the satisfied answer. "Them star men done a good job this time. They're getting more efficienter with every beast, I say."

"Do we *want* it this fresh?" said the first. "Seems like a lot of the good oils coming dribbling and drabbling out of the thing that could be bottled and used and profited from."

"Ah, but what's left must be such quality!" The man kissed his fingers. "Unearthly good. Purest essence of money, trickling into the bosses' pockets—"

And then the bell rang, from the top of the *plan*, mad and loud and on and on.

The whole crowd of workers swayed shoreward as if a gust of wind had bent them. Many day jobbers broke and ran for shore, shouting.

A slow shiver went through the whole length of the beast. At its foot, water splashed up from the drumming of its heel on the *plan*.

The knee team's onlooker flashed by, alone, whom I had thought so professional-looking this morning.

"Down the ropes!" Mister Chopes shouted.

My men, their knees bent to spring into a run, looked to me for the word.

"Back up here!" I megaphoned through the noise. A man fleeing past me clapped his hand to his ear and scowled as he ran on. "We'll wait for the boss!"

But Mister Chopes, tiny on top of the quaking beast, was swinging his arms as if he would scoop us all up and *throw* us toward the head. "We'll go," I said. "On boss's orders. Form up and I'll be the chanter."

And so my men—all of them older than me, because it's the younger and limberer workers who go up top—made two lines in front of me. I used my whistle like a chanter's drum and held them to a rhythm. It was a fast one, but still I kept swinging nearly into the rearmost men—a crutch pace is longer than a normal stride. We passed a man in the water, neither standing nor crouching; excrement ran down his legs and dripped from the hem of his loongy; his wide eyes were fixed on the vast shuddering, looming shadow over us all, and his lips had drawn right back from his big, sticking-out teeth. Beyond him some stretcher men were busy lifting a misshapen, screaming thing with red spikes coming out of it. I tried to watch only the water shooting out flat to the sides when my men's feet hit it.

"Is it electricity?" one of my men asked the knowledgeable one as we ran.

"Is *what* electricity?"

"With the dead frog. Has somebody hit a nerve?"

"A nerve? There's no nerve in a body can make the whole thing shake like that."

When we got to the head end, people in the beast's shadow were calling for help, but no stretcher men ran to them. The harvested hair made a mountain on the *plan*, winched halfway to the hair shed, strands trailing like giant millipedes. The shorn scalp had been taken off, and the sawyers had cut the full oval in the braincase. As we hurried past—we were not close; it only *felt* close because the head was so big—the beast's convulsions made this dish of bone tip slowly outward.

My rhythm went ragged, but my men kept it anyway, bringing *me* back into rhythm, though it should have been me bringing them.

At the top of the *plan* near the steamer sheds was a thick, panicky crowd, all trying not to be the outermost layer. I drew my team up on number 18 *plan*. Our formation was all gone to beggary, but we were together, tight together; none of us was missing, don't worry. From number 17 we must have looked like a row of heads upon a single candy-striped body.

"Is that Mister Chopes?" I looked back down the *plan*. I wanted a boss. I wanted to be in charge of nothing, no one.

"Look at them! And look at those raggedy foot people coming after! Chopes will get commended for this, being so neat and ordered."

"If he doesn't die."

"If we don't all die."

"Look! Look at the stuff inside!"

The bone lid had tipped right out from the beast's head. The head contents sat packed in their cavity. They were supposed to be gray, a purplish gray. Once, I had seen some damaged ones go past, on a lorry; the good ones were shipped across to the Island for sterile processing.

Frog eggs, I thought. Sheep eyes. A lightning storm.

Inside each giant cell floated two masses of blackness, joined by a black bar. Through each cell, and among them, pulsed, flashed, webs, veins, sheets, streaks and sparks of light. Each flicker and pass began yellow, flashed up to white, faded away through yellow again—and so quickly that it took me many flickers to see this, to separate single flashes from the patterns, from the maps the light fast drew, then fast redrew.

"That's the brain," said Trawbrij the chanter. "Those lights must be its thinking. It's alive. They've not killed it properly."

"They've taken their economizing too far," said Mister Chopes. "They've skimped on the drug."

All workers were clear of the beast now, except for the dead, the injured, and two laden stretcher teams splashing up the *plan* through the shallows. The lightning storm flickered and played in the head, now in fine, clear webs at the surface, now deeper and vaguer.

The beast lifted its upper limb, a giant unsteady thing with three clasping digits at the end, from its far side to its head. It felt, with delicate clumsiness, the bald skin above the ear, the angled dish of the skull top.

One of the digits slipped into the cavity, dislodging a single globe there, and whatever tension had held the cells in position was broken. The head contents collapsed like a fruit stack from a market stall. Many rolled right out of the skull, onto the *plan*.

The beast tried to paw the spilt cells back into its skull. Some it retrieved; others it knocked farther away, and they sat gray and lightless on the *plan*. Like a flirty old drunk man fumbling for his fancy Western hat, it groped for its skull dish. It clamped it back onto its head—but crookedly. Several cells were crushed. Their contents burst out; the black barbells cringed and withered; the oils spread upon the seawater; the rest of the filling lay jellied against the casing.

Holding its head together, the beast used a great contraction of its as-yet-uncut abdomen to curve itself up, to roll itself onto its single foot.

*Oh my*, I thought. *It could be mistaken for a person, this one. Like what you see of a person sidling in through a nearly closed door.*

"It can crush the whole town," said Trawbrij. "If it falls that way."

The thing turned, from the sun to the land. There it stood, on its crooked hind limb, loose pieces of gel sliding off it. How many houses high was it, how many hills? Its chest and limbs were patterned with rectangular excavations like a rock quarry; our last unfinished blanket of thigh flesh drooped, dripping. There was a neatly cut cavity where the sex had been, full of drips and runnels like a grotto in the hill caves. Its eye was still sealed, its mouth torn partly open. Brain fluid and matter ran down either side of the gray-stopped nose, in the high sun.

My own head felt light and hollow. *Good!* was the only thought in it. My heart thumped hard, and burned red. Crush the whole town. And the *plan,* too, and everyone on it. Do that.

Three small ornamental picture frames appeared in my mind, around three faces—Jumi's, Dochi's, Jupi's—all looking downward, or to the side. Far overhead, guilt whipped at me as always, but it barely stung. I was deep in my insides; against my cheek and ear some black inner organ, quite separate from my body's functioning, turned and gleamed.

It's only fair.

The beast managed, though one-legged, to take a kind of step. But it sagged toward the missing toe; it gripped and tried to hold itself upright with a toe that wasn't there. Then the weakened knee gave, and the creature jerked and wobbled tremendously above us. And fell—of course it fell. But it fell away from us, stretching itself out across the farther *plans.*

And it lay still.

There were several moments of silence. Nothing moved but eyes.

Then there was an explosion around me, a fountain of striped shirts and shouting mouths, a surge forward.

I knew what they meant; I myself was hot-boweled and shaking with relief. But I didn't surge or shout or leap; I couldn't quite believe. So vast a creature and so strange, and yet the life in it was one-moment-there, next-moment-gone, just as for a dog under a bus wheel, or a chicken that a jumi pulls the neck of. And the world adjusts around it like water; as soon as the fear is gone, as soon as the danger is passed, normalness slips in on all sides, to cover up that any life was ever there.

The *plan* workers rushed in. People came exclaiming into the yards from the town—those who had not seen had certainly heard, had felt the ground jump as the beast collapsed. Women and children crowded at the *plan* gates, and some of the little boys were allowed to run in, because they were not bad luck like the girls and women.

Lots of people—and I was one of these—felt we had to approach the beast, and touch it. Lots of us felt compelled to walk its length and see its motionlessness end to end for ourselves, see its dead face.

"Oh, oh," I said, to no one, as I walked, as I stroked the skin. "All my jupi's careful work."

All the *plans* from 16 to 13 were cracked clean through. The beast had crushed *plan* 13's steamer shed to splinters, its try pots to copper pancakes; it had filled *plan* 12's hair house to the rafters with brain spheres—dead spheres, gray-purplish spheres, spheres that held nothing unexpected.

The stretcher men went to and fro with their serious faces, bearing their serious loads. The bosses withdrew; theirs was the most urgent work. The rest of us could do nothing until the bosses had bargained our jobs back into being, weighed up the damage and set it against the value of the beast and parceled everything out appropriately. Yet we couldn't leave, could only wander dazed, and examine, and exclaim.

Finally, they made us go, because some of the day jobbers

were found snipping pieces of hair, or taking chunks of eyeball or somesuch, and they put ribbons and guards all around the beast and brought the soldiers in to clear the *plans* and keep them clear.

So Jupi and Dochi and I, we walked, still all wobbly, back to our uncrushed home. There was Jumi, waiting to be told, and Jupi described how he had seen it, and Dochi how it had looked from his position up on the forelimb, and I told her yes, between them that was pretty much how it had seemed to me. There was too much to say, and yet none of it would tell properly what had happened, even to people who'd been there, too.

Still, people tried and tried. They came and went—we came and went ourselves—and everyone kept trying.

"How would it be!" said Mavourn.

We were all in the beer shanty by then. I looked down at the thin foam on the beer he had bought me, and smelled the smell, and thought how I didn't want *ever* to like drinking beer.

"How would it be," he said, "to be a beast, to wake up and find yourself chopped half to pieces, and not in the ether anymore, and with no fellow beast to hear your cry?"

"No one can know that, Mavourn," said Jupi. "No one can know how a beast thinks, what a beast feels."

I looked around the table. My colleagues shook their heads, muzzily some of them, with the beer. Some were my family—there was Jupi here, and two distant cousins across from me. I had wanted them all crushed, a few hours ago; what on earth made me want that, in the moment when the beast wavered, and the future was not set?

I could not say. That moment had gone, and the heat in my heart had gone with it. I picked up the beer. I closed my nose to the smell; I looked beyond the far rim so as not to see the slick on the surface from the unclean cup. And I sipped and swallowed, and I put the cup down, and I shook my head along with the other men.

# Into the Clouds on High

"Here." The screen door slapped closed on a gust of cold air. Dad swooshed a bundle of greenery onto the table. "Make something of that."

"What?" Marcus was on the point of finishing his math homework. He'd been looking forward to packing up and going to bed.

"One of your neck-laces," said Dad, shutting the back door. "Though there's no flowers to be had."

Both of them looked at the gerberas in the vase on the table. They were a cheerful, shouty pink. "We can't use those. They're from Josie next door," said Marcus. "She visits just about every day. She'll notice they're gone."

"She'll notice *Mum's* gone a whole lot more."

"I suppose."

The gerberas shouted some more.

"Gotta be better than just green," said Dad.

"They *are* nice and bright."

Dad took the vase to the sink, pulled out the flowers and emptied the water into the plug hole.

Marcus closed the math book and pushed it away. He dragged the whippy green vine stalks toward him. "Are you worried about her, then?"

Dad rinsed the gerbera stems hard under the tap, then wiped them with a tea towel. Mum would have used the kitchen paper. But then, if Mum had been here, the flowers would never have left the vase.

He brought the gerberas back to the table. "Stalks are pretty thick." He eyed Marcus's hands, which were already binding vine stems together. "Won't be a problem, will it?"

"Where will she be, though?"

"Swathes, she told me. I always make her tell me. Just in case of exactly this."

"Do you have a feeling?"

"No. Just a clock." Dad nodded at the microwave. "And a phone that says she can't be reached." He patted the phone in his shirt pocket.

*Can't be reached*—a little stab of fear lit through Marcus's belly. He pushed a gerbera into his face. "These don't have any smell."

Dad sniffed one and pulled his mouth sideways. "It was roses last time, wasn't it?"

"Roses and lavender."

"Lemme think."

Dad went into the bathroom. Marcus began to plait stems, listening to him clink things around in there.

Dad came back with the black bottle of aftershave that always sat behind everything else in the cupboard. "This," he said with a grin. "What I smelt like when we first met. If that doesn't wake her up, I don't know what will." He unscrewed the lid and put it under Marcus's nose.

"Phew. It's stronger than roses and lavender."

"Isn't it, though. We all went round stunk up with the stuff. She liked it back then. All the girls liked it. Or so we told ourselves."

"All right." Marcus was plaiting the green stems, loosely so as to leave room for the gerbera stalks. "Swathes in town, is she? Or Swathes at Eastlands?"

"Town," said Dad. "Or somewhere on the way. Or she might walk in at any minute, and think it's funny that we're worrying. Keep going, though." He set off through the house to the front. Marcus heard him on the porch, on the path, heard the gate. He heard, almost, Dad's head turning as he checked up and down the street. Plait, plait. This would be an interesting wreath—a bit odd-looking, but it would hold together well, these good, strong stalks with their regular sprouts of little leaves along them. In springtime they had yellow flowers, funny-shaped, *like some kind of pea flower,* Mum had described them once, but it was wintertime now, and they weren't even beginning to bud up yet.

Dad came back. "We taking the train in?" said Marcus.

"I thought we'd drive. Be quicker this time of night."

"That's not the way she would've gone, though."

"I figure we'll go up to the railway station, ask if there are any delays on the line, then drive into town and check Swathes."

"You reckon she'd stop the train?"

"Someone'd press the emergency button, for sure. Don't you reckon?"

It was a shame to have to wake Lenny and put her in the baby capsule, but she settled back to sleep pretty quickly once they started driving. Marcus sat in the back with her; he didn't want to take Mum's seat in the front. He just put the gaudy wreath there, in its cloud of aftershave. The smell had got on his hands and stuck there, despite a quick scrubbing with soap-in-a-bottle (lavender, chamomile and orange). Now his hands carried two little clouds of powerful scents, and felt slippery-dry.

It was a long drive; he could have slept, but he wanted to keep Dad company, so he made himself sit up straight and watch the suburbs tumble past, the freeway roll smoothly by. It was a fine, clear night, and everything looked cleaner under only streetlights and neon, kinder, more mysterious. The lights went over Lenny's sleeping face like cloths stroking her, her woolly hat, her fanning eyelashes, her mouth so small and perfect, like the bud of some strange flower, or maybe a fawn's hoofprint in snow. Marcus laid his perfumed hand on the blanket tucked over her stomach, and watched out the windscreen as the night and lights rushed on at them.

\* \* \*

The first time, only Dad had been there—well, Marcus had been, but he'd only been tiny, so he didn't remember any of it. *Scared the gee-willikers out of me*, Dad said. It had been in the laundry, which in the old place—Marcus knew that house as another land, the land of his babyhood, entirely built of Mum and Dad's stories—had been a separate little hut, in the backyard. Dad had gone looking for her, and at first he hadn't checked in the laundry, *because she always made a good racket out there, and once it started, of course, she was dead quiet.* When he found her, he'd called and called, *panicking,* he said, and hung on to her, and finally she'd softened, and floated down and landed beside him, *and let out this big sigh,* Dad said. *She could have been glad to be back or sorry—I couldn't tell. I didn't want to ask. Didn't want to know.*

Marcus had nodded when Dad told him this. That was his instinct, too, to stay closed-lipped about it. Not just to not mention it to anyone except Dad—*that* went without saying—but to not bother Mum, either, with all those questions that bubbled up. They'd had their talk about it; they were taking action; there was no need to bring it up at all, with Mum or with Dad, no need to worry aloud. He'd taught himself to banish the thoughts from his mind if he ever felt too worried, at night or on bad days.

The last time it happened—ages ago, more than a whole year—he'd been right there with her; she'd been pregnant with Lenny then. It was a rainy day, and she was showing him how to make a wreath, from her days in the florist shop. She'd stood up quietly, preoccupied, and he'd kept on poking the lavender stems through the plaited circle of potato vine and making them firm, and the next time he looked up she'd risen and was motionless on the air, and the room was full of a wonderful peace. She'd looked so comfortable. The bump of Lenny wasn't bothering her, wasn't squirming and kicking her under the ribs and making her gasp. Marcus remembered how unafraid he'd been. He could see that she was happy. Not that she was usually *un*happy; it was just that her happiness usually showed in smiles and hugs and such, going out to people; this happiness had flowered inside her, and was held completely within her, and went on and on, smooth, uninterruptible.

And Marcus had been happy, too, because Mum was, and everything felt so right and in place. He'd continued with the flowers, as she'd just taught him. He was rather glad, in fact, that she wasn't there giving him more advice; he was sure he could work it out for himself; he knew what looked right, and how to space the flowers out and mix them evenly.

And then Dad had come in, and the sight of Mum, and the feeling she gave off, certainly hadn't made *him* happy. *How long has she been like this?* He'd thrown his work bag down. If Marcus had been able to be frightened, there within the cloud of Mum's happiness, Dad's face would have frightened him. He'd never seen such wide eyes on him before, such a ragged-looking mouth, like a baby's squaring up to cry. Dad's voice would have frightened him, all high and thin like that.

# Into the Clouds on High

*  *  *

*I suppose you're wondering what that was about, what happened yesterday,* Mum had said to Marcus next day, as they set off for school.

*I suppose I am,* he'd said, because he could see she wanted to talk about it. Although he *hadn't* been wondering. He'd closed it away in his mind along with all the other mysterious things grown-ups did, and he didn't particularly want to take it out and look at it.

*I was being called,* she had said. *From afar. From above.*

He'd waited for more, but none came. Her face had glowed, a little the way it had glowed the day before while she hovered. *Who was calling you?* he'd asked.

Her usual, thinking self had slipped back into place behind her face. Marcus had felt bad to have dismissed the glow from her, the lovely memory. *Who?* she'd repeated. *It wasn't really a who. Or it was so much bigger than, you know, than a single . . . than a* person. *Than any-old-person down here.*

*Why were they calling you?* He'd taken her hand, even though way back at the beginning of kindy he'd told her he was too big to hold hands with her, now that he was a schoolboy.

*I don't know. They thought I could help somehow.*

*Help with what?* And then he'd said something she often said, in quite her own tone of voice: *You've got enough to do.*

She'd looked down and seen how frightened she was making him. *That's right.* She'd squeezed his hand and swung it. *You lot keep me busy enough. And soon there'll be another one of you.*

And she'd patted her Lenny bump, and they'd walked on into the normal day.

But he'd heard her talking to Dad in the kitchen one night as he passed the closed door on the way to the bathroom. *There's a place for me there*, she'd said.

*There's a place for you here!* Dad had said. *With me! With your kids!*

*But I could do so much more from there, and not just for you and Marcus and Lenny. It's bigger. It's more. It's closer to the center of things—I don't know how to explain. It's another level.*

*I want you on this level, darl. I want you to stay here, and to be able to touch and see you, and talk to you, and the kids to be able to, too, and—*

*I won't be going anywhere. I'll still be here. The air you breathe, the water you drink, the weather, the ground—*

Marcus had let the bathroom door close with its usual loud click. He'd crossed to the toilet, and tried to drown out any sound of their voices with as rattling a pee as he could manage.

Dad had been good; he would wink at Marcus if he caught his eye; he would wrestle the same after tea on the lounge-room floor. (*You boys*—Mum would pretend to sound tired—*why do you have to be so* boysie? And Dad, pinning Marcus down and laughing, would say, *We just do, darl. Don't we, mate? Don't we? Don't we?* With every *don't* he would dig his big, strong fingers into Marcus's side. Marcus hated it, loved it, didn't quite know how he felt.)

But Dad had bought the phones, and some of their talk

about the phones, and the rules about them, had leaked out where Marcus could hear. He remembered the importance in Dad's voice: *At all times, all right?* And Mum saying, *I heard you the first time,* crossly, as if Dad was making a fuss about nothing. *It's not going to happen, I tell you. I've got a baby coming.*

*You had a baby* this *time.* They'd both looked at Marcus drawing a stegosaurus for his homework at the kitchen table, and looked away again. *You had a baby* both *times. Does that make a difference to them?*

She'd turned away to the sink, started hissing water onto vegetables to make dinner. *They didn't take me, did they?* she'd said in an only-to-Dad voice. There'd been a hint, in her voice, of wishing, of thinking she'd missed out on something. Marcus's head had popped up and his gaze had quivered like arrows stuck in both of them.

Dad had winked at him, but there'd been no smile in his face to go with it. *Not all the way, no,* he'd said quietly, to the side of Mum's bent head.

*I need you to do something for me, Marcus.*

He and Mum had settled themselves in Eastlands food hall with thick shakes. He'd felt so carefree, just before. It wasn't as if he didn't worry; it was just that the worrying part of his life flowed on separately from the rest, like the Blue Nile river water moving alongside the White. He didn't want them to meet and mix up with each other.

*Dad won't listen,* Mum went on. *He won't do it. He doesn't want to be ready because he doesn't want it to happen. And maybe it won't.*

He tried to read from her face what *she* wanted. She looked around at the other tables, and he examined them, too, the people putting chips into themselves, the food shops sleek and bright, some of the family-owned ones messier with signs and hanging pans and plastic fruit or flowers by their cash registers. He saw that a person who had been lifted off the ground by happiness could be unimpressed with the food hall. For Marcus it was a place of wonders—all he could think about here was how long he could stay, how much he'd be allowed to eat, how much of that could be treats and how much would have to be healthy food.

*But somebody needs to know how to do these things, if it does,* Mum said. He watched her from behind his thick shake, knowing what she was doing, knowing that the shake was a giant white bribe. *Just in case,* Mum said. *I'm not saying it's going to happen tomorrow or anything.*

His hands folded themselves in his lap. It was a lot she was asking of him. Dad wouldn't be happy.

*The way I think of it . . .* She pushed her shake aside and leaned at him, so friendly and comfortable he knew he was going to do what she asked. *The way my luck goes, I'll get you all prepared and nothing'll happen. But if I don't, if I just let things go on as normal, I'll be taken—all the way up, all the way away—and you and Dad'll be left useless. You won't be able to feed yourselves. He'll panic about money. The house'll be filthy.*

He met her eyes, her serious smiling. *Couldn't you just say no?* he said.

Her smile went, and the face behind it was written all over with guilt. He was sorry, straightaway.

*You were there*, she said softly. *You felt some of it, didn't you?*

He nodded, giving in, watching his hands in his lap. One was a tight fist, and the other was wrapped around it—kindly, warningly, or perhaps just to cover the sight of it.

She slid her shake back in front of her and sucked on the straw. She glanced around the food hall, letting the rest of the world back in. *And anyway, they're life skills. It's not as if you'll never use them, even if I stay.*

So now Marcus could cook. Marcus could vacuum and dust and wipe down bench tops, and keep the bathroom clean. Marcus knew how to look after Lenny, what to watch out for, what to make sure she ate, now and in the future, how to get through the illnesses she had to have in order to build her immune system. *She's only small*, Mum had said. *Things can happen very quickly with her, so you need to keep an eye on her, and act fast if it's something dangerous.* He knew all about the little phone and the numbers Mum had put in it. He knew how the money worked, how Dad should move it around when his wage came in, when the bills arrived.

Mum had taught Marcus all this secretly. Dad would have

been upset to find out about it. *He'll learn it soon enough if I do ever go*, Mum had said, that day at Eastlands. *He won't expect you to do it all. But he won't learn it from me, so you'll have to pass it on for us, Marky.* Her cheeks had caved in as she pulled on the shake, it was so thick. *And at the beginning. You might have to do it all for a little while at the beginning. If it ever happens. It might never happen.*

Marcus had been interested to learn how life worked, and pleased to be able to do grown-up things. He'd been proud to know more than other kids at school did, and to keep that knowledge quiet. It was only now, flying through the night toward town, with Dad holding on to his panic in the front seat and Lenny unaware, under his hand, that Marcus felt how sad it was, that he realized he'd been working with Mum toward this moment. Had he made it possible for her to leave by being such a good boy, by carefully soaking up her instructions, by practicing and getting better at things? If he'd been a hopeless cook, or a sloppy cleaner, or an idiot with numbers the way some of the kids at school were, or if he'd just been moody, or if like Dad he'd dug in his heels and refused to believe it was ever going to happen, would she have been unable to go? Should he have made her stay and do the roasts and bills and vacuuming, and the sending of Christmas cards? Should he have folded his arms and stuck out his lip and said, *No, I won't learn?*

But always the little video clip played in his memory, of the rose and lavender wreath coming good in his hands, getting prettier and prettier, while from his floating mum poured down upon Marcus—like the beginnings of a rain shower, like a light sprinkling of gold dust—blessings, well-being, peace and perfect happiness. How could he not want his mum to feel those things? How could he deny them to anyone, let alone her?

Because it was so late, Dad could pull up right outside Swathes. Police tape fluttered across the entrance, and Marcus felt sick at the sight.

"You go and tell them, Dad. I'll get Lenny out." He had a sudden need to busy himself with the mechanics of the baby capsule, with Lenny's blanket and limbs, to support her sleeping head.

Dad came back as he was kicking the car door closed, Lenny in his arms. Dad took her up gently. "Fifth floor, they reckon. She's in the Ladies' loos. There's a million people up there, they say: security, and police, and SES blokes. They're in *lockdown*, they say, that floor. They've kept the staff there and everything. For your mum, eh." He widened his eyes at Marcus, nodded and turned to Swathes's doors, which were all glass, and big silver handles down the sides, and shiny black stone all around, fine grained, with little glints in it. Marcus fetched the wreath out of the front seat, and followed him.

A policewoman lifted the tape for them to duck under; "Ricky here's going to take you up," she said, waving forward a Swathes security guard.

Inside was quiet, alight; people in coveralls, radios spitting and crackling and blurting at their hips, loosely lined the way to the lifts. On the way up Ricky stood with his feet apart, his hands clasped in front of him, and watched the numbers light up one after another. His aftershave was stronger, and sweeter, than the smell of the wreath in Marcus's arms. At the fifth floor he stepped out, and stood aside and waved them out of the lift.

There weren't a *million* people there, but enough eyes turned to Marcus for him to wish he were carrying Lenny, to shield himself from all that attention.

"Across the floor there, mate," Ricky said to Dad. "Through Books to that exit door, and then you turn left."

They set out through the uniforms, through the watching. Some people looked curious, some looked nervous; all of them were sober and unamused, almost as if he and Dad and Lenny had done something wrong. Dad took his great long strides, and Marcus hurried to keep up. Halfway across, as they passed the escalators, he felt a soft buffeting in the air, and the light changed, was more muted and yet more lively. They had stepped within the range of Mum's cloud, of the warmth that fell from her, of the blessings. And they were clear, suddenly, of the crowd; all the eyes were behind them now. The Books section was deserted, two shelves of bright-colored covers leading them to the exit door.

With every step Marcus needed greater willpower to keep walking, as the feeling grew warmer and brighter. It was *strong,* much stronger than that day in the kitchen, and the wonderfulness made it hard for Marcus to think his own thoughts, but with the snippet of his mind that was left to him he knew that he ought to be very worried, though he couldn't worry really, not with all *that* shining at him.

They stepped through the doorway, out of the store proper and into its back halls, cream-lit, linoleum-floored, with doors off to STAIRS and STAFF ONLY and FIRE EXIT—THIS DOOR IS ALARMED. They turned and forged ahead against the resisting warmth, the resisting delight, of the air in the corridor. Witches' hats, and more police tape, and a CLEANING IN PROGRESS sign were clustered at the Ladies' door untidily, as though people hadn't had the time to place them properly.

Dad and Marcus stood at the door. Through everything it was hard for them, as boys, to push open a door like that. The round-headed lady in her skirt stood on it like another kind of guard.

"You okay, champ?" Dad looked down at Marcus through the torrent, around the bundle that was Lenny, sleepily scrambling on his shoulder.

"I'm good," Marcus said, in the flat voice he knew he was supposed to use. He laid his hand on Dad's back, just above his belt, to let him know he was right behind him.

"Let's see, then, eh. What we've got." And Dad pushed open the Ladies' door, and they went in.

The smell of bleach overpowered the aftershave on the wreath for a moment. Both smells were side notes, though, to the outrushing of nectar, of heat, of gold-green changefulness.

"Mum?" Marcus called out softly. What if it wasn't her at all? What if it was not just some other mum, but some other creature completely?

They pushed upstream to the cubicle, stopped at the open door. It *was* Mum, and the relief of finding her filled Marcus as full as he ever needed to be, her good dress with the red swirls on it, her best handbag, her face so restful and pleased, so Mum. She had risen higher than last time; she was farther along in leaving. There was no reason to hope, except that the very air buzzed and poured with hope. It was like a crowd around them shouting for joy, though there were no sounds beyond Dad's and Marcus's own breaths, beyond Lenny's grunts and whimpering as she woke, echoed back from the mirror glass and the wall tiles and the hard floor. It was like looking at the sun, though Marcus's eyes and brain told him that there was no extra light involved in this; he was seeing only his mum uprisen, lit by fluorescent light filtered through white plastic ceiling-squares, nothing out of the ordinary.

"What do you think you're doing, Al?" Dad murmured.

"Um-mah!" said Lenny, turning from his shoulder.

It was difficult to get the words out, and when he did, it sounded as if Marcus lisped, in the inaudible rush of noise. "She's brighter than she was last time," he said.

"Yeah, you better get that neck-lace on her quick."

"I'll have to stand on the loo." Marcus made to go around her, but there was not quite enough room for him to squeeze past the glory of her, on either side.

"Here, I'll put it up," said Dad.

"You want me to hold Lenny?"

"No, she's good." And he held her more firmly against his shoulder, took the ring of flowers from Marcus and reached up and put it over Mum's head. Her hair didn't move where the neck-lace touched it. The flowers settled to her chest, but instead of coming awake as she had last time at their touch, and seeing Marcus and Dad, and easing down out of the air and hugging them all surprised, now she only hung as before, one leg bent as if she were taking a step upward, her face lifted to receive the joy that poured down from above, so that she could re-emit it to people down here—to Marcus and Dad, certainly, but not to them specially. To everyone beyond and around them, to everyone in this place, on this *level*, as she'd said.

Lenny exclaimed and reached up for Mum's face. Her hands, soft and live and harmless, batted and pushed at Mum's ungiving cheeks, Mum's chin, grasped at Mum's earlobe and slid aside on her stony-stiff hair.

"Come on, Al," said Dad. "We're all here waiting for you—me and Marcus and Lenny. Come on home, now. It's a school night. Marky needs to get to bed, eh." And his big hand touched her face, too, and rubbed the collar of her good dress, which should have bent at his touch, but which stayed stiff instead, would not move except to snap, it looked like.

"She's gone too far inside." Marcus hardly heard what he was saying through the joyous turmoil. "Too far away."

"Shh, don't say that," said Dad. "She might hear you; she might think you're giving her permission."

"I don't think she can hear us. I don't think she can hear anything. Not from here. Not anymore."

*Anymore.* He heard himself say that. He knew what it meant, but was unable to mind or fear it. It was just a fact.

Marcus put his arms around the warm curves of Mum's skirt folds, around one of her warm, stone stockinged legs; he laid his cheek against them, though they were the wrong texture, and resisted him. He closed his eyes. It was pointless for Dad to beg and plead and weep the way he did last time. Mum was too entangled, and she was entangling further; her *self* was somewhere else, and she was becoming—within Marcus's arms, under Dad and Lenny's hands—some*thing* else. She flushed hotter and hotter—hotter than normal blood should go. Marcus held tight, hoping she would burn him right up, or tangle him in and take him wherever she was going. The power brimmed and spilled out of her; it poured through Marcus's flesh, through his bones, through his skull and tongue and teeth; Mum shook with the speed and strain, like a car or an aeroplane pushed to its very limits.

"Alice, you *can't*," said Dad, gently, hopelessly. "Please, love, me and these babies? We *need* you, we need you to stay."

But she was gone already, to that other level. And they could not follow; her stiffened clothes, her hard hot skin, were effects of her being drawn through a barrier that would never give way to pleading from this side. Whatever was on the *other* side wanted Mum, and only Mum. It might take them all eventually—it had a larger purpose, which Marcus was too small and too young and too *earthly* to see clearly—but for now, it was only going to perform this small subtraction from the world, this minor addition to the fullness of itself.

"Please, Al? Please?" Marcus could hear that Dad knew he hadn't reached her, and that he wouldn't, ever.

They held on, all three, to what was left of her, the stinging-hot marble of her, the blare of solid light, solid noise, solid needles. She shook in their arms, and cracked soundlessly, cataclysmically; she split up and down and a foreign fire rushed out of her. There was a momentary pain, all the pain of burning alive pressed into a couple of seconds. Lenny shrieked. But then the pain was gone, and a perfect vacancy opened around the four of them, silent, black, cool. *Yes,* thought Marcus, and he tried to pitch himself into it, but it was like that time Dad tried to get him to dive into the deep end of the swimming pool headfirst, with his arms down by his sides. Marcus had bobbed and crouched and laughed at himself, but without his arms to swing up, how could he point himself properly? How could he protect his head?

And as he stood there hugging the shards of her, unable to move, unable to dive, Mum fell, or flew, or melted into the blackness. Marcus stumbled forward, and barely felt the banging of his knees against the rim of the lidded toilet, he was so occupied watching her go, watching her *be taken*.

The invisible light, the inaudible racket, switched off. He

opened his eyes. He and Dad held a rag-Mum between them; he had her skirt end and stocking legs, from which the shoes had clattered to the floor, while Dad held her collapsed upper dress. The handbag teetered where it had *donk*ed onto the toilet lid, and then it tipped and fell to join the shoes.

A little leftover wail eased from Lenny. "Here," said Dad. "Hold this girl." He unclamped Lenny from himself. She drew a shuddering breath and glistened with tears as he transferred her to Marcus. Marcus was glad to take her; she latched hard onto him and pressed her face into his neck. He sat on the toilet lid and held her while Dad folded the clothes, and took down Mum's shopping bags from the hook on the back of the door—the door that someone had kicked or shouldered open, the lock half-broken out of the shattered chipboard and melamine. Dad slid the clothes into the bags like so much other shopping. What had she bought? Marcus wondered. Had she had any clue that she'd never get to use it?

The Ladies' door squealed open. "Y'all right in there?" someone called—one of those tough women in the coveralls, it sounded like, who'd seen all sorts of emergencies in her time.

"Yeah, we're good," Dad called out. He tucked Mum's shoes away in a bag and smiled up at Marcus. "You right there, champ?" he said quietly.

Marcus nodded. He *was* all right, he realized. He felt warm all over, and as if his head was still mildly aflame; he'd been made a torch of, it seemed, by Mum's going.

And she hadn't quite gone; it was true, what she'd said to Dad that night. She hadn't gone so much as she'd kind of exploded, and the powder of her had been sifted all through everything, from Dad's hair to the mirrors over the basins, to the broken chipboard of the door, through the temperature-controlled, freshened air of the bathroom, to the whole Swathes building beyond this room, and outward to the city, and all around that to the countryside and the sea, all their weathers and waters. Every leaf was of her and every grain; every bird and bug had something of Mum in it. It was not as good, and would never be, as having her alive in her real body, falling asleep against her or having her *tut-tut* and busy herself about the house. But it was not as bad as doing without her entirely. He might still talk to her, he felt, and she would hear. If he were to need her badly, she might summon something of her self from its dispersal, and help him be calm and sensible, as she had been, as she'd tried to teach him to be.

Marcus stood and peered into the shopping bags, checked on the floor on either side of the toilet. "Where'd the neck-lace go?"

Dad looked about, too, even under the walls into the cubicles either side. "Huh, what do you know? She took the flowers."

"She doesn't even really *like* gerberas, she told me." Marcus stepped out of the cubicle. A policewoman was standing against the far wall. First a man cop peeped around the tiled divider wall, then an army-looking man with little gold crosses on his collar.

" 'S what you made them into, matey." Dad picked up the shopping bags with a rattle and followed him out. "Worth taking with her up to that wherever-she-went. Heaven or wherever."

"Maybe it was the smell you put on them," said Marcus, and found himself laughing, following the policewoman out of the toilets.

"Ha! Maybe it was! Told you the girls loved it, didn't I?" And Dad clapped a hand on Marcus's shoulder, and left it there as they walked down the corridor, and out into the anxious crowd.

# Night of the Firstlings

Hᴉᴄᴋᴏʀʏ ᴄᴀᴍᴇ ᴅᴏᴡɴ ᴡɪᴛʜ ɪᴛ, same as all the big boys. One minute he was sitting at prayers around the table, the next he hardly looked like himself, he was blotched so red and in between so white.

"Augh." He sounded as if he had no teeth. "It's like something thumped me."

Dawn beside me was suddenly a little stone boy. I took his hand and we sat and could not blink while the fuss was made of Hickory, and for once we didn't mind, so long as they got that livid-patched face out of our sight soon, those swollen-up lips. The blokes are always full of bravado; you cannot tell from them. But Mum with her sharp commands and then her tight silences told us well enough: we ought be very frightened. And we were.

We sat there in the silence of the broken-off prayer. The prophet's children were there, too, though his oldest, Nehemi, was home with the same horror.

"Yer," they said. "It was just like that for ours, too."

" 'Tin't any less awful the second time," whispered Arfur. "They looks like monsters."

Then the prophet himself was back down among us, and he saw their faces and he went to their bench, gathered up little Carris and allowed the others to cling to him. He laughed across at Dawn and me. "Don't worry," he said. "We have the protection. This is what we done all that for."

It didn't help, knowing how serious it had been while we hurried about that day with our secret and our buckets of blood. *If anyone asks you,* Dad had said, *tell them it is a Dukka festival, nothing more.*

*What kinda festival requires good blood slopped about everywhere?* I'd said.

*It's lamb's,* Dad said patiently. *So a spring festival. But only some springs, tell them, because none of them will have seen it before.*

I hoped some of the messier signs we had painted would still work. I remembered adding a few dabs to one of Dawn's efforts while he ran off down the lane calling back that the Ludoes were down there, with their only one boy—but still that made him the eldest, didn't it?, and unable to afford a lamb of their own.

Everyone but Mum and Dad came back down, some of them

quite scared-looking and sweaty. "It is just like with my lad," I heard one say in the stair. "Oh, what a night!"

"Come, people," said the prophet in his prophet voice. "Let us pray thanks that we have the Lord's protection, this fearful night." And they all slid and clambered to sitting around the tables again, and bent their heads.

While he intoned something special and beautiful, nearly singing those words and quite loudly, I bent my head, too, and Dawn leaned against me and I took his hand into my lap. But my attention, which should have been upon God, was wandering up the stair and dabbing about there like the tip of an elephant trunk, sensitive to the least movement. It was unusual that Dad had not come down to play the host while Mum took care of sick Hickory. It was too, too strange that Dawn and I were the only people of our house besides Gramp by the door, while the gathering swayed and responded and clutched its fingers and its brows. I prayed, too, because now I could see there was something to pray for and it wasn't thanks, it was please-please-please. Don't let Hickory's face explode. Please unflop him and roll his eyes back down so as we can see the color in them again. I could not *think* how Mum and Dad would be if Hickory died; too much was possible, too much awfulness.

Once the prayer was sung to a close, the prophet said, "Very well, all youse go to your homes. And those with sons take the peace and strength of Our Lord with you."

And very doubtful and frightened—but not muttering anything because hadn't the prophet seen us correctly through that other stuff, the rust and phylloxera, and the nekkid-lizards all over the place?—everybody shuffled out. Last of all went the prophet himself, who put his thumb to our brows and *winked* at us, and said, "Don't you fear now, through this long night nor no other. For he is with us, God Our God."

"Very well, sir," I said, my mouth obedient though my head boiled with horrors.

Once they'd gone, Dawn looked to me for some answers, but I had none. "I am afraid anyway, whatever he says," I said. "I've never seen anyone so crook as Hickory tonight."

He climbed right into my lap then, though it was a hot night, and put his sticky arms around my neck and his sweaty head against my chest. "What is coming?" he said. "Something is coming. I won't be able to sleep."

"Ushshsh," I said, and held on to him and rocked him as I used to when he was littler. "Don't you worry. Your face is the right color and so is mine."

"For now," he said buzzily into my breastbone. "For *now*."

"Well, now is all we've got and can know about." I hoped I sounded as wise as Mum did when she said it. I knew it was all a matter of the right tone, and the right rhythm of the rocking. Did Mum ever feel so lost, though, as she spoke and held us? Was the world ever so big and dangerous around her?

"Has they all gone!" Dad stumbled out of the stair at the sight. "Where is everyone? They went without their teas!"

"The prophet sent them home," said Dawn quickly, in case Dad felt like dealing out trouble in his worriment.

"Oh." He sat to a bench end and looked about at the nothingness. "I was rather hoping they would stay and console me."

"Got their own lads to unfever," creaked Gramp from the charpoy, "and their own wifes and children to keep calm. How is the lad?"

"He looks dreadful," said Dad. "I have never seen such a thing, to uglify a boy so."

Gramp wheezed—you cannot tell whether he is coughing or laughing most times. Laughing it was, now, because then he said, "When I think the prettiness of the Gypsy prince, all hottened and spoiling."

"I wouldn't wish it on him," said Dad. "On that bastard king himself I would not wish this, watching his boy melt away on his bed. Why can we not just stay as we have done, and work as we have done, and all stay healthy and uncrawled by vermin?"

"What are you saying, son?" says Gramp. "You know well why."

"Oh, I know. Only—" And he sat a moment with his head in his hands like a man praying. "I am tired of the dramas, you know? I never thought I would hear myself say such a thing. But I have children now. All I want is settlement and steadiness in which to watch them grow."

"Which is the whole aim," Gramp said like a stick whacking him, a heavy stick. He was drawn up in such a way, I wondered what was holding him up—just his cloths there?

"I know, Gramp. I know." Dad waved Gramp back down, with his big hands. "I will make us teas," he said. And he closed his mouth and stood.

"Yes, you do that," said Gramp warningly. Dawn looked at him and he glowered back.

Sickness throws out the air of a house; you cannot do what you would usually do. Plus, the prophet had told us to stay in off the streets after sunset, when usually we would be haring about, Dukka and Gypsy together, funneling and screeching up stair and down lane until we got thrown or yelled at, and then in someone's yard, playing Clinks or learning Gypsy letters. *But you cannot be told one from the other like that*, he had said to us. *You must stay to your own houses, you children, with the sign upon the door.*

Mum came down after a while. "I must make our dinner," she said, and she sent Dad up to do the soothing and sponging of Hickory. Which I was grateful for; I had thought she would send me. But he must be seriouser than that. Oh, I didn't want to see him—and at the same time I wanted it very much, to see how much like a monster he was growing. I was very uncomfortable within myself about it all. When I remembered to, I prayed, stirring the foment there for Mum over the fire. But face the truth of it, praying is terribly dull, and who would be Our Lord, sitting up there with the whole world at you, praising and nagging and please-please-please? He must be bored out of his mind as well with it. Some days he must prefer to just go off and count grains of sand. Or birds of the air. Like he does. Like the prophet says he does, who gets to talk direct to him.

# Night of the Firstlings

We ate and it was almost like normal, but after that the light was gone entirely from outside and the usual noises—music trailing down the hill from the Gypsy houses and their laughter from their rooftop parties, and tinkling of glasses and jugs and crashing of plates sometimes—there was none of that.

Every now and again someone would *tap-tap* on our door and whisper to Dad, someone very wrapped—women mostly I think, who were less likely to be stopped and asked their business flittering about so in the evening. Dad would close the door and say, *Baron Hull's boy has it, and all in that region.* Meaning, by *all*, only the biggest boy of each family, we came to know. It was an affliction of the heirs and most precious—very cruel of God, I thought. Dad would go up and tell Mum, and come down again before long, and be restless with us.

Gramp lay abed but did not sleep; there was always the surprisingly alive glitter of his eyes in the middle of his wrappings and covers. No matter how hot the weather, he always was wrapped up warm. *It is because he does not shift his lazy backside,* Mum said, *so his blood sits chilling and spoiling inside him.*

*And I've a right,* he would say. *I've run around enough in my life at barons' becks and calls.*

"Come, Dawn, lie down by me," he said when Dawn drooped at the table. No one wanted to send the boy to bed, or to go themselves. No one wanted to leave the others. Something *was* coming, and no one wanted to be alone when it came.

Dawn went and curled up in the Gramp cloths, and before long slept, and the three of us stayed there, listening to his breaths, which normally would send *me* to sleep quick smartly, but tonight only wound my awakeness tighter, until my eyes took over my face, my ears took over my head, all my thoughts emptied out in expectation of the thing that was on its way. All I had left inside me was Dawn's breath, softly in, softly out, trusting us to look after him while he slept.

I was leaning almost relaxed, making letters in a mist of spilled flour on the table. *Kowt . . . beerlt . . . hamidh.* One day I might have enough to make words, to read Gypsy signage, to get a job writing for them. Opposite me Dad knotted his hands together on the table, watching my clever finger in the flour.

Everything shook a little, that was the first thing.

"Oh, God." Dad looked at the ceiling. "Please do not harm my family, please—" But I ran around and put my hand to his mouth. I climbed up into his lap as Dawn had climbed into mine, because it is comforting to have a child to look after, and even when he dropped his prayer gabble to a whispering, I stopped him with my fingertips.

"Shush, Dad," I said. "Just listen."

Which he did.

How can we sleep, other nights, with that enormous darkness all about, going on and on all the way to the million stars, with all that room in it for winds and clouds, dangers and visitations?

A noise began, so distant at first I wasn't sure of it, but then Dad and Gramp turned their heads different ways, same as me, so I knew it must be: a slow beating that sucked and pushed the air at our ears.

# Night of the Firstlings

Dad held me tighter as it grew, and Gramp curled smaller around Dawn on the charpoy, and his eyes glittered wider. The beating grew outside, and my own pulse thudded like horse-galloping in my chest, and then Dad's heart *thumpa-thump*ed in the back of my head, until I was quite confused which sound was the most frightening. The three of them together, maybe—the two frightened and the one almighty, not caring about either of us, about any of us, four beasts of the town happening to have lifetimes when this thing decided to pass.

Then an air came, gusts and punches of it, with stench upon it and with something else, with a power. It sent through my mind a string of such visions that next time I glimpsed the real world I was under the table, and Dad was clutched hard beside me crying out, and Gramp up there on the charpoy, a lump hardly bigger than Dawn himself, shook over my little brother, his forehead buried in Dawn's sleeping shoulder.

The air of the room was clear, though it ought to've been black, or green and red, beslimed, chockablock with limbs and bits, a-streak with organs and tubing, drippings and sludges. Fouled fleshes and suppurating, torn bodies and assaulted faces, dead or near-dead, stretching in pain, greased with fever or a-shine with blood—the smell, the gusts of it, blossomed these pictures before me. Bury my face in Dad's chest as close as I could, still the air got in, and like a billowing smoke the scenes built one another and streamed and slid and backed up, and gaped and struggled at me.

Next Mum was there with us, Hickory across her lap, sodden,

burning at the center of us. Then Gramp, too, and we were a solid block under the table, all wound around Hickory, keeping the thing off him, keeping the air off, which *whap-whap*ped through the room, which beat outside in the streets, over the town, shaking the night, shaking the world. Our house would fall down on us! We were all as good as dead! *Thank God*, I thought, *at least we are all together*. And I kissed Hickory's hair, which was like wet shoelaces tangled over his head, and I sucked some of the salty sweat out from the strands. He was *so hot*; he was throbbing heat out into us as if he were made of live coals. Gramp was whimpering in *my* shoulder now, and Dawn's head lay sleeping on my hip. I grabbed for Mum's hand, and she held mine so tight in her slippery one it was hard to tell who was in danger of breaking whose bones. The noise blotted out every other noise, louder than the wildest wind and composed, in its beatings, of beating voices, crowds shrieking—terrified or angry or in horrible pain, I could not tell—and the groans of people trampled under the crowd's feet, and the screams of mourners and the wails of the bereaved, all the bereaved there have ever been, all there will ever be, torrents of them, blast after blast.

I woke still locked among their bodies, my dead family's bodies, still under the table. Outside, people ran and screamed still, but they were only tonight's people, only this town's. And they were only—I lay and listened—they were only Gypsies. The only Dukka I heard were calming Gypsies, or hurrying past muttering to each other.

The room still stood around us; it was not crumbled and destroyed or bearing down on the tabletop. The air—I hadn't breathed for a while and now I gasped a bit—the air was only air, carrying no death thoughts, producing no visions.

Dawn sighed on my hip. His ear was folded under his head; I lifted him and smoothed it out, and laid him down again. None of them were dead; what I had thought were the remnants of the beating wind were all their different breaths, countering and crossing one another. Hickory, even. He lay, his normal color so far as I could tell, in the lamplight shadow of Mum and Dad, who were bent forward together as if concentrating very closely on Hickory's sweat-slicked belly, which rose and fell with his even breathing.

It was still hot under there, and so uncomfortable. My right leg, pressed against the floor stones that way, was likely to snap off at the hip, any moment. But it was safe—we were all safe. And it didn't sound safe outside, and I didn't want to *know* what awful things had happened, to make people make those noises. So I put my head down again, half on Hickory's wet-shoelaced skull and half on Gramp's rib-slatted chest, and I closed my eyes and went away again, there in my place in the tangle and dis-comfort of my family.

"I *hate* this place," moaned Dawn, stumbling at Mum's side.

"I know, my darling. Not for long, though. Not for long."

Strange breezes bothered us, hurrying along the channel, dipping from above. The sea had become like a forest either side, with upward streaks like trunks and froth at the top, dancing like wind-tossed leaves. *Shapes* moved in it; these were what terrified Dawn. They terrified all of us, and we hurried; we ran when we could, but it's hard to run with all your belongings bundled on your head, or dragged in a sack behind you, all the gold and silver you've talked out of the Gypsies.

Did you know there are chasms in the sea? Did you know there are mountains and deserts, just as on land? God had granted us a dry path across, but he had not flattened it out for us, had he? The worst had been where we were forced to make a bridge of cloths and clothing, over that bottomless cleft where things churned on ledges and fell away into the darkness, where those clamlike creatures had progressed across the walls, wobbling and clacking.

Dawn tore his hand from Mum's and stopped dead. "I hate this place and I hate the prophet and I *hate* it that we left Gramp behind!"

"You need a beating," said another mum, hurrying past, a child under each arm.

"Move it along, son; don't get in the people's way." A gran swiped at Dawn with her stick.

"Stand to the *side* at least," gasped a bloke bent under a bulging sack.

I ran back and scooped Dawn up. He fought me, but I held on. "We didn't leave Gramp," I said. "He told us to go, remember? I hate it, too, but look—would he have kept ahead of *that?*" I pointed Dawn's screwed-up face to behind us, where the channel was closing like a zip, fitting its teeth back together, swallowing its own foam and somersaulting slowly along itself.

The sight of *that* set him flailing worse. "Lemme down!" he shrieked. "I can run! I'll run, I promise!"

"You better!" I dropped him, and managed to smack his bum before he ran off.

Ahead of us Hickory turned, and quailed at the sight of the channel. "Hurry!" he cried.

"We *are* hurrying. Aren't we, Mum?" Mum was hurrying in a dignified, Mum-like way that wasn't very fast.

Steadying the bundle on her head, she flashed me a smile. "Have faith, daughter; he hasn't made this escape just to drown us all in it."

"Look at it, though!" The advancing foam was tossing up shapes: fishy giants, *trees* of seaweed, something that looked very much like a cart wheel.

"I will not look," she said. "I will only hurry and keep my faith."

"We are coming *last*, Mum! Come on!"

She laughed at me; I could only just hear it over the thunder from behind us, the roar of foam above. "I don't care if I drown now!" she shouted. "At least I will not die enslaved!"

I ran on, a little way ahead of her. Whenever I turned, there she was, proceeding at her own brisk pace and calm. The wall of green-white water caught up to her and tumbled behind her, churning sharks and rocks, dead Gypsies and horses, tentacled things and flights of striped-silver fishes, but never touching her, not with fish or bubble-wrack thrown from its thrashings, not even with a drop of water from the violent masses it had to spare. It towered over us, for we were in the deepest depths of the ocean now. But it did not hurry Mum or overwhelm her, only crept along behind her, a great wild white beast tamed by her tiny happiness.

# Catastrophic Disruption
## of the Head

WHO BELIEVES IN HIS OWN death? I've seen how men stop being, how people that you spoke to and traded with slump to bleeding and lie still, and never rise again. I have my own shiny scars now; I've a head full of stories that goat men will never believe. And I can tell you: with everyone dying around you, still you can remain unharmed. Some boss soldier will pull you out roughly at the end while the machines in the air fling fire down on the enemy, halting the chatter of their guns—at last, at last!—when nothing on the ground would quiet it. I always thought I would be one of those lucky ones, and it turns out that I am. The men who go home as stories on others' lips? They fell in front of me, next to me; I could have been dead just as instantly, or maimed worse than dead. I steeled myself before every fight, and shat myself. But still another part of me stayed serene, didn't it. And was justified in that, wasn't it, for here I am: all in one piece, wealthy, powerful, safe, and on the point of becoming king.

*I have the king by the neck. I push my pistol into his mouth, and he gags. He does not know how to fight, hasn't the first clue. He smells nice, expensive. I swing him out from me. I blow out the back of his head. All sound goes out of the world.*

I went to the war because elsewhere was glamorous to me. Men had passed through the mountains, one or two of them every year of my life, speaking of what they had come from, and where they were going. All those events and places showed me, with their color and their mystery and their crowdedness, how simple an existence I had here with my people—and how confined, though the sky was broad above us, though we walked the hills and mountains freely with our flocks. The fathers drank up their words, the mothers hurried to feed them, and silently watched and listened. I wanted to bring news home and be the feted man and the respected, the one explaining, not the one all eyes and questions among the goats and children.

I went for the adventure and the cleverness of these men's lives and the scheming. I wanted to live in those stories they told. The boss soldiers and all their equipment and belongings and weapons and information, and all the other people grasping after those things—I wanted to play them off against each other as these men said they did, and gather the money and food and toys that fell between. One of those silvery capsules that opened like a seed case and twinkled and tinkled, that you used for talking to your contact in the hills or among the bosses—I wanted one of those.

There was also the game of the fighting itself. A man might lose that game, they told us, at any moment, and in the least dignified manner, toileting in a ditch, or putting food on his plate at the barracks, or having at a whore in the tents nearby. (There were lots of whores, they told the fathers; every woman was a whore there; some of them did not even take your money, but went with you for the sheer love of whoring.) But look, here was this stranger whole and healthy among us, and all he had was that scar on his arm, smooth and harmless, for all his stories of a head rolling into his lap, and of men up dancing one moment, and stilled forever the next. He was here, eating our food and laughing. The others were only words; they might be stories and no more, boasting and no more. I watched my father and uncles, and some could believe our visitor and some could not, that he had seen so many deaths, and so vividly.

*"You are different," whispers the princess, almost crouched there, looking up at me. "You were gentle and kind before. What has happened? What has changed?"*

I was standing in a wasteland, very cold. An old woman lay dead, blown backward off the stump she'd been sitting on; the pistol that had taken her face off was in my hand—mine, that the bosses had given me to fight with, that I was smuggling home. My wrist hummed from the shot, my fingertips tingled.

I still had some swagger in me, from the stuff my drugs man had given me, my going-home gift, his farewell spliff to me, with good powder in it, that I had half smoked as I walked here. I lifted the pistol and sniffed the tip, and the smoke stung in my nostrils. Then the hand with the pistol fell to my side, and I was only cold and mystified. An explosion will do that, wake you up from whatever drug is running your mind, dismiss whatever dream, and sharply.

I put the pistol back in my belt. What had she done, the old biddy, to annoy me so? I went around the stump and looked at her. She was only disgusting the way old women are always disgusting, with a layer of filth on her such as war always leaves. She had no weapon; she could not have been dangerous to me in any way. Her face was clean and bright between her dirt-black hands—not like a face, of course, but clean red tissue, clean white bone shards. I was annoyed with myself, mildly, for not leaving her alive so that she could tell me what all this was about. I glared at her facelessness, watching in case the drug should make her dead face speak, mouthless as she was. But she only lay, looking blankly, redly at the sky.

*She lied to you*, my memory hissed at me.

Ah yes, that was why I'd shot her. *You make no sense, old woman*, I'd said. Sick of looking at her ugliness, I'd turned cruel, from having been milder before, even kind—from doing the old rag-and-bone a favor! *Here I stand*, I said, *with Yankee dollars spilling over my feet. Here you sit, over a cellar full of treasures, enough to set you up in palaces and feed and clothe you queenly the rest of your days. Yet all you can bring yourself to want is this old thing, factory made, one of millions, well used already.*

I'd turned the Bic this way and that in the sunlight. It was like opening a sack of rice at a homeless camp; I had her full attention, however uncaring she tried to seem.

Children of this country, of this war, will sell you these Bics for a packet meal—they feed a whole family with one man's ration. In desperate times, two rows of chocolate is all it costs you. Their doddering grandfather will sell you the fluid for a twist of tobacco. Or you can buy a Bic entirely new and full from such shops as are left—caves in the rubble, banged-together stalls set up on the bulldozed streets. A new one will light first go; you won't have to shake it and swear, or click it some magic number of times. Soldiers are rich men in war. All our needs are met, and our pay is laid on extra. There is no need for us to go shooting people, not for cheap cigarette lighters—cheap and pink and lady-sized.

*Yes, but it is mine*, she had lied on at me. *It was given to me by my son, that went off to war just like you, and got himself killed for his motherland. It has its hold on me that way. Quite worthless to any other person, it is.*

In the hunch of her and the lick of her lips, the thing was of very great worth indeed.

*Tell me the truth, old woman.* I had pushed aside my coat. *I have a gun here that makes people tell things true. I have used it many times. What is this Bic to you? Or I'll take your head off.*

She looked at my pistol, in its well-worn sheath. She stuck out her chin, fixed again on the lighter. *Give it to me!* she said. If she'd begged, if she'd wept, I might have, but her anger set mine off; that was her mistake.

*I lean over the king and push the door button on the remote. The queen's men burst in, all pistols and posturing like men in a movie.*

It was dark under there, and it smelled like dirt and death rot. I didn't want to let the rope go.

*Only the big archways are safe,* she'd said. *Stand under them and all will be well, but step either side and you must use my pinny or the dogs will eat you alive.* I could see no archway; all was black.

I could *hear* a dog, though, panting out the foul air. The sound was all around, at both my ears equally. I knew dogs, good dogs; but no dog had ever stood higher than my knee. From the sound, this one could take my whole head in his mouth.

Which way should I go? How far? I put out my hands, with the biddy's apron between them. I was a fool to believe her; what was this scrap of cloth against such a beast? I made the kissing noise you make to a dog. *Pup? Pup?* I said.

His eyes came alight, reddish—Oh, he was enormous! His tail twitched on the floor in front of me, and the sparse gray fur on it sprouted higher than my waist. He lifted his head—bigger than the whole house my family lived in, it was. He looked down at me over the scabby ridges of his rib cage. Vermin hopped in the beams of his red eyes. His whole starveling face crinkled in a grin. With a gust of butchery breath he was up on his spindly shanks. He lowered his head to me full of lights and teeth, tightening the air with his growl.

A farther dog woke with a bark, and a yet farther one. They set this one off, and I only just got the apron up in time, between me and the noise and the snapping teeth. That silenced him. His long claws skittered on the chamber's stone floor. He paced, and turned and paced again, growling deep and constantly. His lip was caught high on his teeth; his red eyes glared and churned. The hackles stuck up like teeth along his back.

Turning my face aside, I forced myself and the apron forward at him. Oh, look—an archway there, just as the old woman said. White light from the next chamber jumped and swerved in it.

The dog's red eyes were as big as those disks the bosses carry their movies on. They looked blind, but he saw me, he saw me; I *felt* his gaze on me, the way you feel a sniper's, in your spine— and his ill will, only just held back. I pushed the cloth at his nostrils. Rotten-sour breath gusted underneath at me.

But he shrank as the old woman had told me he would, nose and paws and the rest of him; his eyes shone brighter, narrowing to torch beams. Now I was wrapping not much more than a pup, and a miserable wreck he was, hardly any fur, and his skin all sores and scratches.

135

I picked him up and carried him to the white-flashing archway, kicking aside coins; they were scattered all over the floor, and heaped up against the red-lit walls. Among them lay bones of dog, bird, sheep, and some of person—old bones, well gnawed, and not a scrap of meat on any of them.

I stepped under the archway and dropped the mangy dog back into his room. He exploded out of himself, into himself, horribly huge and sudden, hating me for what I'd done. But I was safe here; that old witch had known what she was talking about. I turned and pushed the apron at the next dog.

He was a mess of white light, white teeth, snapping madly at the other opening. He smelt of clean, hot metal. He shrank to almost an ordinary fighting dog, lean, smooth-haired, strong, with jaws that could break your leg bone if he took you. His eyes were still magic, though, glaring blind, bulging white. His heavy paws, scrabbling, pushed paper scraps forward; he cringed in the storm of paper he'd stirred up when he'd been a giant and flinging himself about. As I wrapped him, some of the papers settled near his head: American dollars. *Big* dollars, three-numbered. Oh these, *these* I could carry, these I could use.

For now, though, I lifted the dog. Much heavier, he was, than the starving one. I slipped and slid across the drifts of money to the next archway. Beyond it the third dog raged at me, a barking firestorm. I threw the white dog back behind me, then raised the apron and stepped up to the orange glare, shouting at the flame dog to settle; I couldn't even hear my own voice.

He shrank in size, but not in power or strangeness. His coat seethed about him, thick with waving gold wires; his tongue was a sprout of fire, and white-hot arrow tips lined his jaws. His eyes, half-exploded from his head, were two ponds of lava, rimmed with the flame pouring from their sockets—clearly they could not see, but my bowels knew he was there behind them, waiting for his chance to cool his teeth in me, to set me alight.

I wrapped my magic cloth around him, picked him up and shone his eye light about. The scrabbles and shouting from the other dogs behind me bounced off the smooth floor, lost themselves in the rough walls arching over. Where was the treasure the old biddy had promised me in this chamber, the richest of all the three?

The dog burned and panted under my arm. I walked all around, prodding parts of the walls in case they should spill jewels at me or open into treasure rooms. I reached into cavities, hoping to feel bars of gold, giant diamonds—I hardly knew what.

All I found was the lighter the old biddy had asked me to fetch, the pink plastic Bic, lady-sized. And an envelope. Inside was a letter in boss writing, and attached to that was a rectangle of plastic, with a picture of a foreign girl on it, showing most of her breasts and all of her stomach and legs as she stood in the sea edge, laughing out of the picture at me. Someone was playing a joke on me, insulting my God and our women instead of delivering me the treasure I'd been promised.

I turned the thing over, rubbed the gold-painted lettering that stood up out of the plastic. Rubbish. Still, there were all those Yankee dollars, no? Plenty there for my needs. I pocketed the Bic and put the rubbish back in the hole in the wall. I crossed swiftly to the archway, turned in its safety and shook the dog out of the cloth. Its eyes flared wide, and its roar was part voice, part flame. I showed it my back. I'd met real fire that choked and cooked people—this fairy fire held no fear for me.

Back in the white dog's chamber, I stuffed my pack as full as I could, every pocket of it, with the dollars. It was *heavy*! It and the white fighting dog were almost more than I could manage. But I took them through and into the red-lit carrion cave, and I subdued the mangy dog there. I carried him across to where rope end dangled in its root-lined niche, and I pulled the loop down around the bulk of the money on my back, and the dog still in my arms, and hooked it under myself.

There came a shout from above. Praise God, she had not run off and left me.

*Yes!* I cried. *Bring me up!*

When she had me well off the floor, I cast the red-eyed dog out of the apron cloth. He dropped; he ballooned out full-sized, long-shanked. He looked me in the eye, with his lip curled and his breath fit to wither the skin right off my face. I flapped the apron at him. *Boo,* I said. *There. Get down.* The other two dogs bayed deep below. Had they made such a noise at the beginning, I never would have gone down.

And then I was out the top of the tree trunk and swinging from the branch, slower now than I'd swung before, being so much heavier. The old woman stood there, holding me and my burden aloft, the rope coiling beside her. She was stronger than I would have believed possible.

*Do you have it?* She beamed up at me.

*Oh, I have it, don't worry. But get me down from here before I give you it. I would not trust you as far as I could throw you.*

And she laughed, properly witchlike, and stepped in to secure the rope against the tree.

*She is not the first virgin I've had, my little queen, but she fights the hardest and is the most satisfying, having never in her worst dreams imagined this could happen to her. I have her every which way, and she urges me on with her screams, with her weeping, with her small fists and her torn mouth and her eyes now wide, now tight-closed squeezing out tears. The indignities I put her through, the unqueenly positions I force her into, force her to stay in, excite me again as soon as I am spent. She fills up the air with her pleading, her horror, her powerless pretty rage, for as long as she still has the spirit.*

I left the old woman where she lay, and I took her treasure with me, her little Bic. I walked another day, and then a truck came by and picked me up and took me to the next big town. I found a bank, and had no difficulty storing my monies away in it. There I learned what I had lost when I put the sexy-card back in the cave wall, for the bank man gave me just such a one, only plainer. The card was the key to my money, he said. I should show the card to whoever was selling to me, and through the magic of computers the money would flow straight out of the bank to that person, without me having to touch it.

*Where is a good hotel?* I asked him when we were done. *And where can I find good shopping, like Armani and Rolex?* These names I had heard argued over, as we crouched in foxholes and behind walls waiting for orders; I had seen them in the boss magazines, between the pages of the women some men tortured themselves with wanting, during the many boredoms of the army.

The bank man came out with me onto the street and waved me up a taxi. I didn't even have to tell the driver where to go. I sat in the back seat and smiled at my good fortune. The driver eyed me in the mirror.

*Watch the road,* I said. *You'll be in big trouble if I get hurt.*

*Sir,* he said.

At the hotel I found that I was already vouched for; the bank had telephoned them to say I was coming and to treat me well.

*First,* I said, *I will have a hot bath, a meal, and some hours' sleep. I've traveled a long way. Then I will need clothes, and this uniform to be burned. And introductions. Other rich men. Rich women, too; beautiful women. I'm sure you know the kind of thing I mean.*

When I was stuffing my pack full of dollars underground, I could not imagine ever finding a use for so much money. But then began my new life. A long, bright dream it was, of laughing friends, and devil women in their devil clothes, and wonderful drugs, and new objects and belongings conjured by money as if by wizardry, and I enjoyed it all and thoroughly. Money lifts and floats you, above cold weather and hunger and war, above filth, above having to think and plan—if any problem comes at you, you throw a little money at it and it is gone, and everyone smiles and bows and thanks you for your patronage.

That is, until your plastic dies. *Then* I understood truly what treasure I'd rejected when I left that card in the third cave. There was no more money behind my card; that other card, with the near-naked woman on it, behind *that* had been an endless supply; *that* card would never have died. I had to sell my apartment and rent a cheaper place. Piece by piece I sold all the ornaments and furniture I'd accumulated, to pay my rent. But even the worth of those expensive objects ran out, and I let the electricity and the gas go, and then I found myself paying my last purseful for a month's rent in not much more than an attic, and scrounging for food.

I sat one night on the floor at my attic window, hungry and glum, with no work but herding and soldiering to turn my fortunes around with. I went through my last things, my last belongings left in a nylon backpack too shabby to sell. I pulled out an envelope, with a crest on it of a hotel—ah, it was those scraps from the first day I had come to this town, with all my money in my pack. These were the bits and pieces that the chamber boy had saved from the pockets of my soldiering clothes. *Shall I throw these away, sir?* he'd said to me. *No,* I told him. *Keep them to remind me how little I had before today. How my fortunes changed.*

*Ha!* I laid the half spliff on my knee. A grain fell out of the tip. That had been a good spliff, I remembered, well laced with the fighting powder that made you a hero, that took away all your fear.

*And you!* I took out the pink lighter, still fingerprinted with the mud of that blasted countryside.

*Ha!* One last half spliff would make this all bearable. A few hours, I would have, when nothing mattered, not this house, not this hunger, not my own uselessness and the stains on my memory from what I had done as a rich man, and before that as a soldier. And then, once it was done . . . Well, I would just have to beggar and burgle my way home, wouldn't I, and take up with the goats again. But why think of that now? I scooped the grain back into the spliff and twisted the end closed. I flicked the lighter.

Some huge thing, rough, scabby, crushed me to the wall. I gasped a breath of sweet-rotten air and near fainted. Then the thing adjusted itself, and I was free, and could see, and it was that great gray spindly dog from the underground cave, turning and turning on himself in the tiny space of my attic, sweeping the beams of his red movie-disk eyes about, at me, at my fate and circumstances.

I stared at the lighter in my hand. A long, realizing sound came out of me. So the lighter was the key to the dogs! You flicked it, they came. And see how he lowered his head and his tail in front of me, and looked away from my stare. He was mine, in my power! I didn't need some old apron-of-a-witch to wrap him in and tame him.

Sweat prickled out on me, cold. I'd nearly left this Bic with the old biddy, in her dead hand, for a joke! Some other soldier, some civilian scavenger, some child, might have picked it up and got this power! I'd been going to fling it far out into the mud-land around us, just to laugh while she scrabbled after it. I'd been going to walk away laughing, my pack stuffed with the money I'd brought up from below, and the old girl with nothing.

I looked around the red-lit attic, and out the window at the patched and crowded roofs across the way, dimming with evening. I need never shiver here again; I need never see these broken chimneys or these bent antennae. Now I *enjoyed* the tweaking of the hunger pangs in my belly, because I was about to banish them forever, just as soon as I summoned that hot golden dog with his never-dying money card.

I clicked the lighter three times.

And so it all began again, the dream, the floating, the powders and good weed, the friends. They laughed again at my stories of how I had come here from such a nowhere. For a time there my family and our goats had lost their fascination, but now they enthralled these prosperous people again, as travelers' tales had once bewitched me around the home fires.

*I catch the queen by the shoulders. One of her men dives for his gun. I shoot him; his eye spouts; he falls dead. The queen gives a tiny shriek.*

I heard about the princess from the man who fitted out my yacht. He had just come from the tricky job of making lounges for the girl's prison tower, which was all circular rooms.

*Prison?* I said. *The king keeps his daughter in a prison?*

# Yellowcake

*You haven't heard of this?* he laughed. *He keeps her under lock and key, always has. He's a funny chap. He had her stars done, her chart or whatever, right when she was born, and the chart said she'd marry a soldier. So he keeps her locked up so's this soldier won't get to her. She only meets people her parents choose.*

*Oh, does she?* I thought, even as I laughed and shook my head with the yacht man.

That night when I was alone and had smoked a spliff, I had the golden dog bring her. She arrived asleep, his back a broad bed for her, his fire damped down for her comfort. He laid the girl on the couch nearest the fire.

She curled up there, belonging as I've never belonged in these apartments, delicate, royal, at peace. She was like a carved thing I'd just purchased, a figurine. She was beautiful, certainly, but not effortfully so, as were most women I had met since I'd come into my wealth. It was hard to say how much of her beauty came from the fact that I knew she was a princess; her royalty seemed to glow in her skin, to be woven into her clothing, every stitch and seam of it considered and made fit. Her little foot, out the bottom of the nightdress, was the neatest, palest, least walked-upon foot I had ever seen since the newborn feet of my brothers and sisters. It was a foot meant for an entirely different purpose from my own, from most feet of the world.

Even in my new, clean clothes, like a man's in a magazine, I felt myself to be filth crouched beside this creature. These hands of mine had done work, these eyes had seen things that

144

she could never conceive of; this memory was a rubbish heap of horrors and indignities. It was one thing to be rich; it was quite another to be born into it, to be royal from a long line of royalty, to have never lived anything but the palace life.

The princess woke with the tiniest of starts. Up and back from me she sat, and she took in the room, and me.

*Have you kidnapped me?* she said, and swallowed a laugh.

*Look at your eyes*, I said. Her whole face was bright awake, and curious, and not disgusted by me.

*Perhaps your name?* she said gently. Her nightwear was modest in covering her neck to ankle, but warmth rushed through me to see her breasts so clearly outlined inside the thin cloth.

I made myself meet her eyes. *Can I serve you somehow? Are you hungry? Thirsty?*

*How can I be?* said the princess, and blinked. *I am asleep and dreaming. Or stoned. It smells very strongly of weed in here. Where was I before?*

I brought a tray of pretty foods from the feast the golden dog had readied. I sat beside her and poured us both some of the cordial. I handed it to her in the frail stemmed glass, raised mine to her and drank.

*I shouldn't touch it*, she whispered. *I am in a story; it will put me under some spell.*

*Then I am magicked, too*, I said, and raised again the glass I'd sipped from, pretending to be alarmed that half was gone.

She laughed, a small, sweet sound—she had very well kept

teeth, just like the magazine women, the poster women. Then she drank.

*Now, tell me, what is all this?* I said of the tray. *These little things here—they must be fruit by their shape, no? But why are they so small?*

She ate one, and it clearly pleased her. *Who is your chef?* she said, with a kind of frown of pleasure.

*He is a secret,* I said, for I could hardly tell her that a dog had made this feast.

*Of course.* She took another of the little fruits, and ate it, and held her fingers ready to lick, a delicate spread fan.

She touched her fingers to a napkin, then put the tray aside. She knelt beside me, and leaned through the perfume of herself, which was light and clean and spoke only quietly of her wealth. *Who are you?* she said, and she put her lips to mine, and held them there a little, her eyes closing, then opening surprised. *Do you not want to kiss me?*

*I sat with my fellows in the briefing room at the barracks. Up on the movie screen, foreign actors were locked together by their lips. Boss soldiers groaned and hooted in the seats in front of us. We giggled at the screen and at the men. "And they call us tribals," said my friend Kadir, who later would be blown to pieces before my eyes. "Look at how wild they are, what animals! They cannot control themselves."*

The princess was poised to be dismayed or embarrassed. *Oh, I do want to,* I said, *but how is it done?* For, except for my mother in my

146

childhood, I had never kissed a woman—even here in my rich-man life—in a way that was not somehow a violence upon her.

*So handsome, and you don't already know?* But she taught me. She was gentle, but forceful; she pressed herself to me, pushed me (with her little weight!) down onto the couch cushions. I was embarrassed that she must feel my desire, but she did not seem to mind, or perhaps she did not know enough to notice. She crushed her breasts against me, her belly and thighs. And the kissing—I had to breathe through my nose, for she would not stop, and there was no room for my breath with all her little lively tongue, and her hair falling and sliding everywhere, and eventually I dared to put my hands to her rounded bottom and pull her harder against me, and closed my eyes against the consequences.

*Hush,* she said over me at one point, rising off me, her hair making a slithering tent around our heads and shoulders, all dark gold. Her breasts hung forward in the elaborate frontage of the nightgown—I was astonished by their closeness; I covered them with my hands in a kind of swoon.

I told her what I was, in the night, over some more of that beautiful insubstantial food. I told her about the old woman, and the dogs; I showed her the Bic. *That is all I am,* I said. *Lucky. Lucky to have lived, lucky to have come into this fortune, lucky to have you before me. I am not noble and I have no right to anything.*

*Oh,* she said, *but it is all luck, don't you see?* And she knelt up and held my face as a child does, to make you listen. *My own family's wealth, it came about from the favors of one king and one bishop, back in the fourteenth century. You learn all the other, all the speaking and manners and how to behave with people lower than yourself; it can be learned by goatherds and by soldiers just as it can by the farmers my family once were, the loyal servants.*

She kissed me. *Certainly you look noble,* she whispered, and smiled. *You are my prince, be sure of that.*

She dazzled me with what she was, and had, and said, and what she was free from knowing. But I would have loved her just for her body and its closeness, how pale she was, and soft, and intact, and for her face, perfect above that perfection, gazing on me enchanted. She was like the foods she fancied, beautiful nothingness, a froth of luxury above the hard, real business of the world, which was the machinery of war and missiles, the flying darts and the blown dust and smoke, the shudder in your guts as the bosses brought in the air support, and saved you yet again from becoming a thing like these others, pieces of bleeding litter tossed aside from the action, their part in the game ended.

*With the muzzle of the pistol, I push aside the queen's earring—a dangling flower or star, made of sparkling diamonds, a royal heirloom. I press the tip in below her ear, fire, and drop her to the carpet. It's all coming back to me, the efficiency. "Bring me the prince!" I cry.*

The women of the bosses' world, they are foul beautiful creatures. They are devils that light a fire in the loins of decent men.

# Catastrophic Disruption of the Head

One picture is all you need, and such a picture can be found on any boss soldier's wall in the barracks; my first time in such a place, all my fellows around me were torn as I was between feasting their eyes on the shapes and colors taped to the walls, and uttering damnation on the bosses' souls, and laughing—for it was ridiculous, wasn't it, such behavior? The taping itself was unmanly, a weakness—but the posturing of the picture girls, I hardly knew how to regard that. I had never seen *faces* so naked, let alone the out-thrustingness of the rest of their bodies. I was embarrassed for them, and for the boss men who looked upon these women, and longed for them—even as the women did their evil work on me, and woke my longings, too.

We covered our embarrassment by pulling the pictures down, tearing one, but only a little, and by accident. We put them in the bin, where they were even less dignified, upside down, making their faces of ecstasy and scorn, or animal abandon. We looked around in relief, the walls bare except for family pictures now. Someone opened a bedside cupboard and found those magazines they have. Around the group of us they went, and we yelped and laughed and pursed our mouths over them, and some tried to whistle as the bosses whistled; I did not touch one at all, not a single page, but I saw enough to disgust and enliven me both for a long time to come.

Someone raised his head, and we all listened. Engines. *Land Rover! They are coming!* And we scrambled to put the things back, made clumsy by our laughter and our fear.

*This is the best one! Take this one with us!*

*Straighten them! Straighten them in the cupboard, like we found them!*

I remember as we ran away, and I laughed and hurried with the rest, another part of me was dazed and stilled by what I had seen, and could not laugh at all. Those women would show themselves, *all* of themselves, parts you had never seen, and did not want to—or did you?—to any man, any; they would let themselves be put in a picture and taped up on a wall for any man's eyes. I was stunned and aroused; I felt so dirtied that I would never be clean, never the man I had been before I saw what I had seen.

And now I was worse, myself, even than those bosses. I lived, I knew, an unclean life. I did not keep my body pure, for marriage or any other end, but only polluted myself and wasted my good seed on wanton women, only poisoned myself with spliffs and powders and liquors.

It is very confusing when you can do anything. You settle for following the urge that is strongest, and call up food, perhaps. Then this woman smiles at you, so you do what a man must do; then another man insults you, so you pursue his humiliation. While you wait for a grander plan to emerge in your head, a thousand small choices make up your life, none of them honorable.

It is much easier to take the right path when you only have two to choose from. Easiest of all is when you are under orders, or under fire; when one choice means death, you can make up your mind in a flash.

These things, about the women and my impurity, I would

not tell anyone at home. This was why my family stayed away from the greater, the outer world; this was why we hid in the mountains. We could live a good life there, a clean life.

*Buzzz*. I go to the wall and press the button to see out. Three men stand at the door downstairs. They wear suits, old-fashioned but not in a dowdy way. *You thought you had run ahead of us*, say the steep white collars, the strangely fastened cuffs, and the fit, the cut of those clothes; even a goat boy can hear it. *But our power is sunk deep, spread wide, and knotted tight into the fabric of all things*.

The closest one takes off his sunglasses. He calls me by my army name. I fall back a little from the screen. "Who are you and what do you want?"

"We must ask you some questions, in the name of His Majesty the King," he says. He's well fed, the spokesman, and pleased with himself, the way boss soldiers are, the higher ranks who can fly away back to Boss Land if things get too rough for them.

"I've nothing to say to any king," I say into the grille. How is he onto me so quickly? Does *he* have magic dogs as well?

"I have to advise you that we are authorized to use force."

I move the camera up to see beyond them. Their car gleams in the apartment's turning circle, with the royal crest on the door. Six soldiers—spick-and-span, well armed, no packs to weigh them down if they need to run—are lining up alert and out of place on the gravel. Behind them squats an armored vehicle, a prison on wheels.

I pull the sights back down to the ones at the door. I wish I had wired those marble steps the way the enemy used to. I itch for a button to press, to turn them to smoke and shreds. But there are plenty more behind them. By the look of all that, they know they're up against more than one man.

I buzz them in to the lobby. In the bedroom I take the pistol from my bedside drawer. In the sitting room lie the remains of the feast, the spilled throw rug that the princess wrapped herself in as she talked and talked last night. I pick up the Bic and click it twice. "Tidy this up," I say into the bomb blast of silver, and he picks up the mess in his teeth and tosses it away, and goggles at me for more orders. He could deal with this whole situation by himself if I told him. But I'm not a lazy man, or a coward.

The queen's men knock at the apartment door. I get into position—it feels good, that my body still knows how. "Shrink down, over there," I say to the silver dog. The light from his eyes pulses white around the walls.

Three clicks. "Fetch me the king!" I shout before the gold dog has time to properly explode into being, and they arrive together, the trapped man jerking and exclaiming in the dog's jaws. He wears a nice blue suit, nice shoes, all bespoke as a king's clothes should be.

The knocking comes again, and louder. The dog stands the king gently on the carpet. I take the man in hand—not roughly, just so he knows who's running this show. "Sit with your friend," I say to the dog, and he shrinks and withdraws to the window, his flame fur seething. The air is strong with their spice and hot metal, but it won't overpower me; I'm cold and clever and I know what to do.

I lean over the king and push the door button on the remote. The queen's suits burst in, all pistols and posturing. Then they see me; they aren't so pleased with themselves then. They scramble to stop. The dogs stir by the window and the scent tumbles off them, so strong you can almost see it rippling across the air.

"You can drop those," I say. The men put up their hands and kick their guns forward.

I have the king by the neck. I push my pistol into his mouth, and he gags. He doesn't know how to fight, hasn't the first clue. He smells nice, expensive.

"Maybe he can ask me those questions himself, no?" I shout past his ear. I swing him around to where he will not mess me up so much. "Bring me the queen!" I shout to the golden dog, and blow out the back of the king's head. The noise is terrific; the deafness from it wads my ears.

The queen arrives stiff with fear between the dog's teeth. Her summery dress is printed with carefree flowers. Her skin is as creamy as her daughter's; her body is lean and light and has never done a day's proper work. I catch her to me by the shoulders. One of the guards dives for his gun. I shoot him in the eye. The queen gives a tiny shriek and shakes against me.

The dogs' light flashes in the men's wide eyes. "Please!" mouths their captain. "Let her go. Let her go."

I can feel the queen's voice, in her neck and chest, but her lips are not moving. She's trying to twist, trying to see what's left of the king.

"What are you saying, Your Majesty?" I shake her, keeping my eyes on her men. "Are you giving your blessing, upon your daughter's marriage? Perhaps you should! Perhaps I should make you! No?" My voice hurts in my throat, but I only hear it faintly.

I take her out from the side, quickly so as not to give her goons more chances. I drop her to the carpet. It's all coming back to me, the efficiency.

"The prince!" I command, and there he is, flung on the floor naked except for black socks, his wet man wilting as he scrambles up to face me. I could laugh, and tease him and play with him, but I'm not in that mood. He's just an obstacle to me, the king's only other heir. My gaze fixes on the guards; I push my pistol up under his jaw and I fire. The silent air smells of gun smoke and burnt bone.

"Get these toy boys out of here," I shout to the dogs, even more painfully, even more faintly. "Put the royals back, just the way they are. In their palace, or their townhouse, or their brothel, or wherever you found them. My carpet, and my clothes here—get the stains off them. Don't leave a single clue behind. Then go down and clear the garden, and the streets, of all those men and traffic."

It's not nice to watch the dogs at work, picking up the live men and the dead bodies both, and flinging them like so many rags, away to nothing. The filthy dog, the scabbed one—why must *he* be the one to lick up the blood from the carpet, from the white leather of the couch? Will he lick me clean, too? But my clothes, my hands, are spatter-free already; my fingertips smell of the spiciness of the golden dog, not the carrion tongue of the mangy one.

The carpet and couch are as white as when I chose them from the catalogue; the room begins to look spacious again without all the intruders.

I open the balcony windows to let out the smell of death and shooting. Screams come up from the street, and a single short burst of gunfire. A soldier flies up past me, his machine gun separating from his hands. They go up to dots in the sky, and neither falls back down.

By the time I reach the balcony railing, all is gone from below except people fleeing from what they've seen. The city lies in the bright morning, humming with its many lives and vehicles. I spit on its peacefulness. Their king is dead, and their prince. Soon they'll be ruled by a goatherd, all those suits and uniforms below me, all those bank men and party boys and groveling shop owners. Everyone from the highest dignitary to the lowliest beggar will be at my disposal, subject to my whim.

I stride back into the apartment, which is stuffed fat with the dogs. They shrink and fawn on me, and shine their eyes about.

"I want the princess!" I say to the golden one, and he grins and hangs out his crimson tongue. "Dress her in wedding finery, with the queen's crown on her head. Bring me the king-crown, and the right clothes, too, for such an occasion. A priest! Rings! Witnesses! Whatever papers and people are needed to make me king!"

Which they do, and through everyone's confusion and my girl's delight—for she thinks she's dreaming me still, and the news hasn't yet reached her that she is orphaned—the business is transacted, and all the names are signed to all the documents that require them.

But the instant the crown is placed on my head, my rage, which was clean and pure and unquestioning while I reached for this goal, falters. Why should I want to rule these people, who know nothing either of war or of mountains, these spoiled fat people bowing down to me only because they know I hold their livelihoods—their very lives!—in my hands, these soft-living men, these whore women, who would never survive the cold, thin air of my home, who would cringe and gag at the thought of killing their own food?

"Get them out of here," I say to the golden dog. "And all this nonsense. Only leave the princess—the queen, I should say. Her Majesty."

And the title is bitter on my tongue, so lately did I use it for her mother. King, queen, prince and people, all are despicable to me. I understand for the first time that the war I fought in, which goes on without me, is being fought entirely to keep this wealth safe, this river of luxury flowing, these chefs making their glistening fresh food, these walls intact and the tribals busy outside them, these lawns untrampled by jealous mobs come to tear down the palaces.

And she's despicable, too, who was my princess and dazzled me so last night. Smiling at our solitude, she walks toward me in that shameful dress, presenting her breasts to me in their silken tray, the cloth sewn close about her waist to better show how she swells above and below, for all to see, as those dignitaries saw just now, my wife on open display like an American celebrity woman in a movie, like a porn queen in a sexy-mag.

I claw the crown from my head and fling it away from me. I unfasten the great gold-encrusted king-cape and push it off; it suffocates me, crushes me. My girl watches, shocked, as I tear off the sash and brooches and the foolish shirt—truly tear some of it, for the shirt fastenings are so ancient and odd it cannot be removed undamaged without a servant's help.

Down to only the trousers, I'm a more honest man; I can see, I can *be*, my true self better. I take off the fine buckled shoes and throw them hard at the valuable vases across the sitting room. The vases tip and burst apart against each other, and the pieces scatter themselves in the dogs' fur as they lie there intertwined, grinning and goggling, taking up half the room.

The princess—the queen—is half-crouched, caught mid-laugh, midcringe, clutching the ruffles about her knees and looking up at me. "You are different," she says, her child face insulting, accusing, above the cream-lit cleft between her breasts. "You were gentle and kind before," she whispers. "What has happened? What has changed?"

Yellowcake

I kick aside the king-clothes. "Now you," I say, and I reach
for the crown on her head.

*My mother stirs the pot as if nothing exists but this food, none of us
children tumbling on the floor fighting, none of the men talking and
taking their tea around the table. The food smells good, bread baking,
meat stewing with onions.*

*It is a tiny world. The men talk of the larger, outer one, but
they know nothing. They know goats, and mountains, but there
is so much more that they can't imagine, that they will never see.*

I shower. I wash off the blood and the scents of the princess,
the bottled one and the others, more natural, of her fear above
and of her flower below that I plucked—that I *tore*, more truth-
fully, from its roots. I gulp down shower water, lather my hair
enormously, soap up and scrub hard the rest of me. Can I ever be
properly clean again? And once I am, what then? There seems
to be nothing else to do, once you're king, once you've treated
your queen so. I could kill her, could I not? I could be king
alone, without her eyes on me always, fearful and accusing. I
could do that; I've got the dogs. I could do anything. (I lather
my sore man parts—they feel defiled, though she was my wife
and untouched by any other man—or so she claimed, in her
terror.)

I rinse and rinse, and turn off the hissing water, dry myself
and step out into the bedroom. There I dress in clean clothes,
several layers, Gore-Tex the outermost. I stuff my ski cap and

gloves in my jacket pockets, my pistol to show my father that my tale is true. I go into my office, never used, and take from the filing drawers my identifications, my discharge papers—all I have left of my life before this, all I have left of myself.

Out on the blood-smeared couch my wife-girl lies unconscious or asleep, indecent in the last position I forced on her. She's not frightened anymore, at least, not for the moment. I throw the ruined ruffled thing, the wedding dress, to one side, and spread a blanket over her, covering all but her face. I didn't have to do any of what I did. I might have treated her gently; I might have made a proper marriage with her; we might have been king and queen together, dignified and kind to each other, ruling our peoples together, the three giant dogs at our backs. We could have stopped the war; we could have sorted out this country; we could have done anything. Remember her fragrance, when it was just that light bottle-perfume? Remember her face, unmarked and laughing, just an hour or so ago as she married you?

I stand up, away from what I did to her. The fur-slump in the corner rises and becomes the starving gray, the white bull-baiter, the dragon dog with his flame coat flickering around him, his eyes fireworking out of his golden mask face.

"I want you to do one last thing for me." I pull on my ski cap. The dogs whirl their eyes and spill their odors on me.

I bend and put the pink Bic in the princess's hand. Her whole body gives a start, making me jump, but she doesn't wake up.

159

I pull on my gloves, heart thumping. "Send me to my family's country," I say to the dogs. "I don't care which one of you."

Whichever dog does it, he's extremely strong, but he uses none of that strength to hurt me.

The whole country's below me, the war *there*, the mountains *there*, the city flying away back *there*. I see for an instant how the dogs travel so fast: the instants themselves adjust around them, make way for them, squashing down, stretching out, whichever way is needed for the shape and mission of the dog.

Then I am stumbling in the snow, staggering alongside a wall of snowy rocks. Above me, against the snow-blown sky, the faint lines of Flatnose Peak on the south side and Great Rain on the north curve down to meet and become the pass through to my home.

The magic goes out of things with a snap like a passing bullet's. No giant dog warms or scents the air. No brilliant eye lights up the mountainside. My spine and gut are empty of the thrill of power, of danger. I'm here where I used to imagine myself when we were under fire with everything burning and bleeding around me, everyone dying. Snow blows like knife-slashes across my face; the rocky path veers off into the blizzard ahead; the wind is tricky and bent on upending me, tumbling me down the slope. It's dangerous, but not the wild, will-of-God kind of dangerous that war is; all I have to do to survive here is give my whole mind and body to the walking. I remember this walking; I embrace it. The war, the city, the princess, all the technology and money I had, the people I knew—these all become things I once dreamed, as I fight my frozen way up the rocks, and through the weather.

*"I should like to meet them," she says to me in the dream, in my dream of last night when she loved me. She sits hugging her knees, unsmiling, perhaps too tired to be playful or pretend anything.*

*"I have talked too much of myself," I apologize.*

*"It's natural," she says steadily to me, "to miss your homeland."*

I edge around the last narrow section of the path. There are the goats, penned into their cave; they jostle and cry out at the sight of a person, at the smells of the outside world on me, of soap and new clothing.

In the wall next to the pen, the window shutter slides aside from a face, from a shout. The door smacks open and my mother runs out, ahead of my stumbling father; my brothers and sisters overtake them. My grandfather comes to the doorway; the littler sisters catch me around the waist and my parents throw themselves on me, weeping, laughing. We all stagger and fall. The soft snow catches us. The goats bray and thrash in their pen with the excitement.

"You should have sent word!" my mother shouts over all the questions, holding me tightly by the cheeks. "I would have prepared such a feast!"

"I didn't know I was coming," I shout back. "Until the very last moment. There wasn't time to let you know."

"Come! Come inside, for tea and bread at least!"

Laughing, they haul me up. "How you've all grown!" I punch my littlest brother on the arm. He returns the punch to my thigh and I pretend to stagger. "I think you broke the bone!" And they laugh as if I'm the funniest man in the world.

We tumble into the house. "Wait," I say to Grandfather as he goes to close the door.

I look out into the storm, to the south and west. Which dog will the princess send? The gray one, I think; I hope she doesn't waste the gold on tearing me limb from limb. And when will he come? How long do I have? She might lie hours yet, insensible.

"Shut that door! Let's warm the place up again!" Every sound behind me is new again, but reminds me of the thousand times I've heard it before: the dragging of the bench to the table, the soft rattle of boiling water into a tea bowl, the chatter of children.

"You will have seen some things, my son," says my father too heartily—he's in awe of me, coming from the world as I do. He doesn't know me anymore. "Sit down and tell us them."

"Not all, though, not all." My mother puts her hands over the ears of the nearest sister, who shakes her off annoyed. "Only what is suitable for women and girl folk."

So I sit, and sip the tea and soak the bread of home, and begin my story.

# Ferryman

"WRAP YOUR PA SOME LUNCH up, Sharon," says Ma.

"What, one of these bunnocks? Two?"

"Take him two. And a good fat strip of smoke. And the hard cheese, all that's left. Here's his lemon." She whacks the cork into the bottle with the flat of her hand.

I wrap the heavy bottle thickly, so it won't break if it drops. I put it in the carry-cloth and the bunnocks and other foods on top, in such a way that nothing squashes anything else.

"Here I go."

Ma crosses from her sweeping and kisses my right cheek. "Take that for him and this for you." She kisses my left. "And tell him about those pigeon; that'll give him spirit till this evening."

"I will." I lift the door in the floor.

I used to need light; I used to be frightened. Not anymore.

Now I step down and my heart bumps along as normal; I close the lid on myself without a flinch.

I start up with "The Ballad of Priest and Lamb." The stairway is good for singing; it has a peculiar echo. Also, Ma likes to hear me as I go. "It brightens my ears, your singing," she says, "and it can't do any harm to those below, can it?"

Down I go. Down and down, down and round, round and round I go, and all is black around me and the invisible stone stairs take my feet down. I sing with more passion the lower I go, and more experimenting, where no one can hear me. And then there begins to be light, and I sing quieter; then I'm right down to humming, so as not to draw attention when I get there.

Out into the smells and the red twilight I go. It's mostly the fire river that stinks, the fumes wafting over from way off to the right before its flames mingle with the tears that make it navigable. But the others have their own smells, too. Styx water is sharp and bites inside your nostrils. Lethe water is sweet as hedge roses and makes you feel sleepy.

Down the slope I go to the ferry, across the velvety hell-moss badged here and there with flat red liverworts. The dead are lined up in their groups looking dumbly about. "Once they've had their drink," Pa says, "you can push them around like tired sheep. Separate them out, herd them up as you desire. Pile them into cairns if you want to! Stack them like faggots—they'll stay however you put them. They'll only mutter and move their heads side to side like birds."

The first time I saw them, I turned and ran for the stairs. I was only little then. Pa caught up to me and grabbed me by the back of my pinafore. "What the blazes?" he said.

"They're horrible!" I covered my face and struggled as he carried me back.

"What's horrible about them? Come along and tell me." And he took me right close and made me examine their hairlessness and look into their empty eyes, and touch them, even. Their skin was without print or prickle, slippery as a green river stone. "See?" said Pa. "There's nothing to them, is there?"

"Little girl!" a woman called from among the dead. "So sweet!"

My father reached into the crowd and pulled her out by her arm. "Did you not drink all your drink, madam?" he said severely.

She made a face. "It tasted foul." Then she turned and beamed upon me. "What lovely hair you have! Ah, youth!"

Which I don't. I have thick, brown, straight hair, chopped off as short as Ma will let me—and sometimes shorter when it really gives me the growls.

My dad had put me down and gone for a cup. He made the woman drink the lot, in spite of her faces and gagging. "Do you want to suffer?" he said. "Do you want to feel everything and scream with pain? There's a lot of fire to walk through, you know, on the way to the Blessed Place."

"I'm suffering now," she said, but vaguely, and by the time she finished the cup, I was no longer visible to her—nothing was. She went in among the others and swayed there like a tall, thin plant among plants. And I've never feared them since, the dead. My fear dried up out of me, watching that woman's self go.

Here comes Pa now, striding up the slope away from the line of dead. "How's my miss, this noontide? How's my Scowling Sarah?"

Some say my dad is ugly. I say his kind of work would turn anyone ugly, all the gloom and doom of it. And anyway, I don't care—my dad is my dad. He can be ugly as a sackful of bumholes and still I'll love him.

Right now his hunger buzzes about him like a cloud of blowflies. "Here." I slip the carry-cloth off my shoulder. "And there's two fat pigeon for supper, in a pie."

"Two fat pigeon in one fat pie? You set a wicked snare, Sharon Armstrong."

"You look buggered." I sit on the moss beside him. "And that's a long queue. Want some help, after?"

"If you would, my angel." *Donk,* says the cork out of the bottle. Pa's face and neck and forearms are all brown wrinkled leather.

He works his way through a bunnock, then the meat, the cheese, the second bun. He's neat and methodical from first bite to last sup of the lemon.

When he's done, he goes off a way and turns his back to pee into the lemon bottle, for you can't leave your earthly wastes down here or they'll sully the waters. He brings it back corked and wrapped and tucks it into the carry-cloth next to a rock on the slope. "Well, then."

I scramble up from the thick, dry moss and we set off down the springy slope to the river.

A couple of hours in, I'm getting bored. I've been checking the arrivals, sending off the ones without coin and taking the coin from under those tongues that have it, giving the paid ones their drink and checking there's nothing in their eyes, no hope or thought or anything, and keeping them neat in their groups with my stick and my voice. Pa has poled hard, across and back, across and back. He's nearly to the end of the queue. Maybe I can go up home now?

But in his hurry Pa has splashed some tears onto the deck. As he steps back to let the next group of the dead file aboard, he slips on that wetness, and disappears over the side, into the woeful river, so quickly he doesn't have time to shout.

"Pa!" I push my way through the slippery dead. "No!"

He comes up spluttering. Most of his hair has washed away.

"Thank God!" I grab his hot, wet wrist. "I thought you were dead and drowned!"

"Oh, I'm dead all right," he says.

I pull him up out of the river. The tears and the fire have eaten his clothes to rags and slicked the hairs to his body. He looks almost like one of *them*. "Oh, Pa! Oh, Pa!"

"Calm yourself, daughter. There's nothing to be done."

"But look at you, Pa! You walk and talk. You're more yourself than any of these are theirs." I'm trying to get his rags decent across his front, over his terrible bald willy.

"I must go upstairs to die properly." He takes his hands from his head and looks at the sloughed-off hairs on them. "Oh, Sharon, always remember this! A moment's carelessness is all it takes."

I fling myself at him and sob. He's slimed with dissolving skin, and barely warm, and he has no heartbeat.

He lays his hand on my head and I let go of him. His face, even without hair, is the same ugly, loving face; his eyes are the same eyes. "Come." He leads the way off the punt. "It doesn't do to delay these things."

I follow him, pausing only to pick up the carry-cloth in my shaking arms. "Can you not stay down here, where we can visit you and be with you? You're very like your earthly form. Even with the hair gone—"

"What, you'd have me wander the banks of Cocytus forever?"

"Not forever. Just until—I don't know. Just not now, just not to lose you altogether."

His hand is sticky on my cheek. "No, lovely. I must get myself coined and buried and do the thing properly. You of all people would know that."

"But, Pa—!"

He lays a slimy finger on my lips. "It's my time, Sharon," he says into my spilling eyes. "And I will take my love of you and your mother with me, into all eternity; you know that."

I know it's not true, and so does he. How many dead have we seen, drinking all memory to nowhere? But I wipe away my tears and follow him.

We start up the stairs, and soon it's dark. He isn't breathing;

all I can hear is the sound of his feet on the stone steps, which is unbearable, like someone tonguing chewed food in an open mouth.

He must have heard my thoughts. "Sing me something, Scowling Sarah. Sing me that autumn song, with all the wind and the birds in it."

Which I'm glad to do, to cover the dead-feet sounds and to pretend we're not here like this, to push aside my fear of what's to come, to keep my own feet moving from step to step.

We follow the echoes up and up, and when I reach the end of the song, "Beautiful," he says. "Let's have that again from the very start."

So I sing it again. I have to break off, though, near to the end. The trapdoor is above us, leaking light around its edges.

"Oh, my pa!" I hold his terrible flesh and cry. "Don't come up! Just stay here on the stair! I will bring you your food and your drink. We can come down and sit with you. We will *have* you, at least—"

"Go on, now." He plucks my arms from his neck, from his waist, from his neck again. "Fetch your mother for me."

"Just, even—" My mind is floating out of my head like smoke. "Even if you could stay for the pigeon! For the pie! Just that little while! I will bring it down to you, on the platter—"

"What's all this noise?" The trapdoor opens. Ma gives a shout of fright seeing Pa, and yes, in the cooler earthly light his face is—well, it is clear that he is dead.

"Forgive me, wife," says his pale, wet mouth. His teeth show through his cheeks, and his eyes are unsteady in his shiny head. "I have gone and killed myself, and it is no one's fault but my own." He has no breath, as I said. The voice, I can hear in this realer air, comes from somewhere else than his lungs, somewhere else, perhaps, than his body completely.

Ma kneels slowly and reaches, slowly, into the top of the stair.

"Charence Armstrong," she weeps at him, her voice soft and unbelieving, "how could you do this?"

"He fell in the Acheron, Ma; he slipped and fell!"

"How could you be so stupid?" she tells him gently, searching the mess for the face she loves. "Come to me."

"As soon as I step up there I am dead," he says. "You must come down to me, sweet wife, and make your farewells."

There's hardly the room for it, but down she comes onto the stairs, her face so angry and intense it frightens me. And then they are like the youngest of lovers in the first fire of love, kissing, kissing, holding each other tight as if they'd crush together into one. She doesn't seem to mind the slime, the baldness of him, the visibility of his bones. The ragged crying all around us in the hole, that is me; these two are silent in their cleaving. I lean and howl against them and at last they take me in, lock me in with them.

Finally, we untangle ourselves, three wrecks of persons on the stairs. "Come, then," says my father. "There is nothing for it."

"Ah, my husband!" whispers Ma, stroking his transparent cheeks.

All the workings move under the jellified skin. "Bury me with all the rites," he says. "And use real coin, not token."

"As if she would use token!" I say.

He kisses me, wetly upon all the wet. "I know, little scowler. Go on up, now."

When he follows us out of the hole, it's as if he's rising through a still water-surface. It paints him back onto himself, gives him back his hair and his clothes and his color. For a few flying moments he's alive and bright, returned to us.

But as his heart passes the rim, he stumbles. His face closes. He slumps to one side, and now he is gone, a dead man taken as he climbed from his cellar, a dead man fallen to his cottage floor.

We weep and wail over him a long time.

Then, "Take his head, daughter." Ma climbs back down into the hole. "I will lift his dear body from here."

The day after the burial, he walks into sight around the red hill in company with several other dead.

"Pa!" I start toward him.

He smiles bleakly, spits the obolus into his hand and gives it to me as soon as I reach him. I was going to hug him, but it seems he doesn't want me to.

"That brother of mine, Gilles," he says. "He can't hold his liquor."

"Gilles was just upset that you were gone so young." I fall into step beside him.

He shakes his bald head. "Discourage your mother from him; he has ideas on her. And he's more handsome than I was. But he's feckless; he'll do neither of you any good."

"All right." I look miserably at the coins in my hand. I can't tell which is Pa's now.

"In a moment it won't matter to me." He puts his spongy hand on my shoulder. "But for now, I'm counting on you, Sharon. You look after her for me."

I nod and blink.

"Now, fetch us our cups, daughter. These people are thirsty and weary of life."

I bring the little black cups on the tray. "Here, you must drink this," I say to the dead. "So that the fire won't hurt you."

My father, of course, doesn't need to be told. He drinks all the Lethe water in a single swallow, puts down the cup and smacks his wet chest as he used to after a swig of apple brandy. Up comes a burp of flowery air, and the spark dies out of his eyes.

I guide all the waiting dead onto the punt. I flick the heavy mooring rope off the bollard and we slide out into the current, over the pure, clear tears-water braided with fine flames. The red sky is cavernous; the cable dips into the flow behind us and lifts out ahead, dripping flame and water. I take up the pole and push it into the riverbed, pushing us along, me and my boatload of shades, me and what's left of my pa. My solid arms work, my lungs grab the hot air, my juicy heart pumps and pumps. I never realized, all the years my father did this, what solitary work it is.

# Living Curiosities

I WENT TO DULCIE PEPPER'S TENT and slapped my hand onto her table, palm up.

"I'm sorry, Nonny-girl. Looking at that, you'll not grow another inch." She reached for her pipe. "Clawed your way through that queue, did you?"

"Have you had *anyone* tonight?"

"One strange young man. How about you Ooga-Boogas?"

"A family or two, and a man—oh, probably the same man as you. Very clean clothes, and uncomfortable in them."

"Uncomfortable in his *skin*, that one. He gave me the shivers, he did."

"Spent a long time in with the pickle jars, then came out and stood well back from us, did not try to speak. Even Tommy could not get so much as a *Good evening* out of him, though he did nod when greeted. Mostly just stared, though, from one to another of us and back again. Twice around, he went, as if he did not want to miss a thing."

"Hmm." Dulcie leaned back in her shawl-draped chair and put her humdrum boots up next to the crystal ball. She is not so much a crystal gazer; the ball is mostly for atmosphere. She does complicated things with her own set of cards that she will not say where they came from, and mainly and bestly she reads hands. Not just palms, but *hands*, for there is as much to be read from fingertips as from the palm's creases, she says. "Where was I, then, last time?"

"You had just told Mister Ashman as much as you could, about them ghosts."

"Oh yes, which was not very much, and all confused, as is always the case when you come to a moment of choice and possibilities. It's as bad as not seeing anything sometimes; really, you could gain as much direction consulting a person of only common sense. But perhaps those are rarer than I'm thinking, rarer even than fortune-tellers. Anyway, John Frogget comes by."

"John Frogget? What was he doing there?" I tried to disguise that his name had spilled a little of my tea.

"Well, he must quarter somewhere, too, no, for the winter? That was the year his pa died. He said he would not go to Queensland and duke it out with his brothers for the land. He waited closer to spring and then went up a month or two and rabbited for them. Made a tidy pot, too. All put away in the savings bank nicely—there's not many lads would be so forethoughtful."

I tried to nod like one of those commonsense people. I nearly always knew whereabouts John Frogget was, and if I didn't know where, I imagined. Right now I could hear the *pop-pop* of someone in his shooting gallery, alongside the merry-go-round music. So he would be standing there in the bright-lit room, all legs and folded arms and level gaze, admiring if the man was a good shot, and careful not to show scorn or amusement if he was not. "So what did Frogget do, then, about your ghosts?"

"Well, he tried to shoot them, of course—we asked him. At first he was too frightened. Such a steady boy, you would not credit how he shook. He could not believe it himself. So at first his shots went wide. But then he calmed himself, but blow me if it made any difference. *Look*, he says, *I am aimed direct in the back of the man's head or at his heart, but the shot goes straight through the air of him*. He made us watch, and *ping!* and *zing!* and *bdoing!* It all bounced off the walls and the two of them just kept up their carry-on, the ghost man cursing and the woman a-mewling same as ever. And then *rowr-rowr-chunka-chunka* the *thing* come down the alley like always, and poor Frogget—we had not warned him about that part!" Laughter and smoke puffed out of her, and she coughed. "We had to just about scrape him off the bricks with a butter knife, he was pressed so flat! Oh!"

"Poor lad," I said. "You and Mister Ashman at least were used to it."

"I know. We knew we would come to no harm. Ashman had stood on that exact spot many times and been run down by the ghost horses and the ghost cart, like I told you. It might have whitened his hair a little more, the sensations of it, but he were never crushed, by any means. Standing there in the racket with his hands up and *Stand to! Begone, now!* As if he were still right center of the ring, and master of everything." She watched the memory and laughed to herself.

"So Ashman could not boss the ghosts away, and Frogget could not shoot them. So what did you do then?" I did not mind what she said, so long as she kept on talking, so long as Mrs. Em stayed away, with her *Come, Nonny-girl, there is some public waiting*. Some days, some nights, I could bear the work, if it could be called work, being exhibited; others, I felt as if people's eyes left slug trails wherever they looked, and their remarks bruises, and their whispers to each other little smuts and smudges all over us. The earth men and the Fwaygians and the Eskimoos were too foreign and dark to notice, and Tommy was too much a personality to ever take offense, but I, just a girl, and pale, and so much smaller than them all . . . All I wanted was to go back to my quarters, lock my door and wash myself of the public's leavings, and then hurry away, under cover of carriage or train blind or only night's darkness from anywhere I would be spotted as one of Ashman's Museum pieces.

"There was nothing we *could* do," said Dulcie, "so we just put up with it, most that winter. I went and asked them, you know? I told them how tiresome they were, how he was never going to get his money out of her, that they were dead, didn't they realize? That they were going to die from this cart coming along in a minute. It was like talking to myself, as if I were mad or drunk myself. You just had to wait, you know? The terrible noise—I cannot describe, somehow, how awful it was. There was more to it than noise. It shook you to your bones, and then to something else; it was hard to keep the fear off you. And sometimes four or five times a night, you know? And Ashman and me clutching each other like babes in the wood with a big *owl* flying over, or a *bat,* or a *crow* carking."

"It is hard to imagine Ashman fearful—"

Dulcie sat up, finger raised, eyes sliding. We listened to the bootsteps outside that paused, that passed. "Him again," she whispered.

"Who again?"

"Mister Twitchy." She tapped the side of her head.

"How can you *know,* from just that?"

She put a finger to her lips, and he passed again, back down toward the merry-go-round. That was where I would go, too, were I a free woman, a customer, alone and uncomfortable. There was nothing like that pootle-y music, that colored cave, those gliding swan coaches and those rising and falling ponies, the gloss of their paint, the haughtiness of their heads, the scenes of all the world—Paris! Edinburgh Castle! The Italian Alps! You could stand there and warm your heart at the sight, the way you warm your hands at a brazier. You could pretend you were anywhere and anyone—tall, slender, of royal birth, with a face like The Lovely Zalumna, pale, mysterious, beautiful at the center of her big, round frizz of Circassian hair.

"Ashman. Fearful." Dulcie brought us both back from our listening. "Yes, I know, he is so commanding in his manner. But he was sickening for something, you see, all that while. I don't know whether the ghosts were the cause or just an aggravation. But it came to midwinter and he were confined to his bed, and we hardly needed to light the fire, his own heat kept the room so warm. The great stomach of him, you know? I swear some nights I saw it glowing without benefit of the lamp! And the delirium! It was all I could do some nights to keep him abed. And one night I had shooed him back to his bed so many times—I had *wrestled* him back, if you can imagine! Well, up he stands, throws off his nightshirt, which is so wet you could wring it out and fill a teacup easy with the drippings. Up he stands, runs to the window, tears the curtains aside, and there's the moon out there hits him like a spotlight. And he says—oh, Non, I cannot tell you for laughing now, but at the time, I tell you, he raised gooseflesh on me! *I am Circus*, he says—to the moon, to the lane, to the ghosts, to me? I don't know. To himself! *I am Circus*, he announces, in his ringmaster voice. *I am all acts, all persons, all creatures, all curiosities, rolled into one*. And I says—it was cruel, but I had been up all night with him—I says, '*Roll*' is right, *you great dough lump of a man. Get back into bed*. And he turns around and says to me, *Dulce, I have seen a great truth; it will change everything. I need hire no one; I need pay nothing; I can do it all myself, with no squabbles nor mutinies nor making ends meet!*

"*What is that?* I say, pushing him away from the window, for should anyone come down the lane, hearing his shouts and wondering who needs help down there, who needs taking to the madhouse, they will see him all moonlit there, naked as a baby and with his hair all over the place. He'd be mortified, I'm thinking, if he were in his right sense. Let alone they might *take* him to the madhouse! Anyway, on he goes. He can ride a horse as well as any equestrian, he says, now that he knows how the horse feels, what it thinks. He can *be* the horse. He can multiply himself into *many* horses, he says, as many as we need—"

I love it when Dulcie gets to such a stage in a story, her face all open and lively, her eyes full of the sights she's uttering, as if none of this were here, the tent or the Gypsy tat or the cold night and strange town outside. She goes right away from it all, and she takes me with her, the way she describes everything.

"And he's just about to show me what he can do on the trapeze—*I will have a suit*, he says, *all baubles and bugle beads like The Great Fantango, and I will swing and I will fly!*

"And he's going for the window and I'm fighting him and wondering should I scream for help if he gets it open? Will he push *me* out if I'm in his way? And how much do I care for him, anyway? Am I willing to have my brains dashed out in an alleyway on the chance it will give him pause and save his life?

"And up goes the window and the wind comes in, *smack!*, straight from the South Pole, I tell you, Nonny, and a little thing like Tasmania was never going to get in its way! It took the breath out of me, and the room was an icebox, like *that*."

She snaps her dry fingers. "But you would think it was a . . . a zephyr, a tropical breeze, for all it stops Ashman. *I will fly!* he says, *I will fly!* And he pushes the sash right up and he's hands either side the window and his foot up on the sill. *With the greatest of ease!* he shouts."

Here Dulcie stopped and looked crafty. "And now I must fill my pipe," she said calmly.

"Dulcie Pepper, I hate you!" I slid off the stool and ran around and pummeled her while she laughed. "You *always*— You *torture* a girl so!"

"How can it matter?" she said airily, elbowing my fists away. " 'Tis all long over now, and you *know* he lives!"

"If I could reach, I would strangle you." I waved my tiny paws at her and snarled, rattling my throat the way I had learned from the Dog Man.

"And then you would never hear the end, would you?" she said smugly. "Unless you ran and asked Ashman himself."

Gloomily I went back to my stool and watched her preparations. Faintly bored, I tried to seem, and protested no more, for the more I minded the longer she would hold off.

At first she moved with a slowness calculated to irritate me further, but when I kept my lips closed, she tired of the game and gathered and tamped the leaf shreds into the black pipe. Before she even lit it, she went on. "And right at that minute, as if they were sent to save his life, that drunken ghost starts below: *Where's me dashed money, you flaming dash-dash?* And his woman starts to her crying. *What do you mean you haven't got it?*

he says. Cetra, cetra. It was funny, I could *see* the gooseflesh on Ashman. It ran all over and around him like rain running over a puddle, you know, little gusts of it. And back he steps, and takes my hands and makes me sit down on the bed. *Dulce*, he says, *I see it so clearly.* And it ought to have made me laugh, it were so daft, but the way he said it, suddenly it seemed so true, you know? Because he believed it so, he almost *made* it true. And also, the ghosts in the lane, they will turn things serious; it was very hard to laugh and be light with those things performing below."

"What did he say, though?"

She struck her pipe alight, delaying herself at this sign of my eagerness. "He says"—and she narrowed her eyes at me through the first thick-curling smoke—"*Inside every Thin Man, he says, there is a Fat Lady trying to be seen, and to live as that Fat Lady, and fetch that applause. Inside every Giant there is a Dwarf, inside every Dwarf a Giant. Inside every trapeze artist a lion tamer lives, or a girl equestrian with a bow in her hair, and inside every cowboy is a Wild Man of Borneo, or a Siam Twin missing his other half.*"

Sometimes I was sure Dulcie Pepper had magic, the things she did with her voice, the force of her eyes, her smokes and scents and fabrics, and the crystal ball sitting there like another great eye in the room, or the moon, or a lamp, and the way my scalp crept, some of the things she said. *Inside every Dwarf a Giant*—and there she had drawn me; Mister Ashman had seen me in his delirium and here was Dulcie to tell me, that all of us freaks and ethnologicals felt the same, and Chan the Chinee

Giant was the mirror of me, both sizes yearning toward the middle, toward what seemed long-limbed and languid to me, miniature and delicate to Chan.

"A Fat Lady inside every Thin Man?" I said doubtfully, but when I thought about it, it was very like what Chan and I wanted, the opposite of what we were.

Dulcie shrugged. "So he said. *But inside me,* he said, *because I am a businessman and a white man and a civilized man and a worker with my mind and not my hands, inside me is the lot of them, blackamoor and savage, rigger and cook and dancing girl on horseback. And now that I know the trick,* he says, *now that I have the key, I can open the door; I can bring them all out! I am a circus in my own self. Do you see how convenient this is?*

"Which, of course, I *could* . . ." She laughed, and examined the state of the burning tobacco. "And it would, certainly, have saved a lot of bother, just the two of us tripping around the place."

"But it wasn't *true!*" I said. "It wasn't *possible!*"

"Exactly. And then I could hear the cart coming, the horses and the rumbling wheels, and I thought, Good, this will put an end to this nonsense. And—"

A man shouted outside, and boys, and in a moment feet ran up the hill toward us, boys' anxious voices, excited. Dulcie started up, swept to the tent door and snatched it aside as the last of Hoppy Mack's sons passed by. "What's up, you lads?" she called out.

"Dunno. Something has happened in Frogget's."

Instantly I was locked still on my seat, a dwarf girl of ice. Nothing functioned of me but my ears.

"*He's* not shot, is he?" Thank God for Dulcie, who could ask my question for me!

"No, he's all fine," said the boy, farther away now. " 'Twas him told us to go for Ashman."

That unlocked me. I hurried out past Dulcie, and she followed me down the slope of grass flattened into the mud by Sunday's crowd and still not recovered two days later.

John Frogget had doused the lamps around his sign and was prowling outside the booth door, all but barking at people who came near. "No!" he said to Ugly Tom. "Give the man some dignity. He is not one of your pickles, to be gawped at for money." Which, as there were a number of ethnologicals coming from the Museum tent—as there was *me*, but could he see me yet?— was a mite insensitive of him. But he was upset.

"What has happened, John?" said Dulcie sensibly. I retreated aflutter to her elbow, looking John up and down for blood.

"A man has shot himself with my pistol."

"Shot himself dead?"

"Through the eye," said John, nodding.

"Through the *eye*!" breathed Dulcie as John turned from us to the others, gabbling at him. She grasped my shoulder. "Nonny, do you think? Could it possibly?"

"What?" I said, rather crossly because she hurt me with her

big hand, so tight, and her weight. But her face up there was like the beam from the top of a lighthouse, cutting through my irritations.

"No," I said.

*Uncomfortable in his skin, that one.*

"No." I liked a good ghost story, but I did not want to have looked upon a man living his last hour. "He was *rich*! He had the best-cut coat! And new boots!" I pled up to Dulcie, grasping her skirt like an infant its mother's.

"Here he comes!" said Sammy Mack, and down the hill strode Ashman in his shirtsleeves, but with his hat on. I could not imagine him naked and raving and covered in gooseflesh, as Dulcie had described him.

"What's up, Frogget?" He pushed through the onlookers—he didn't have to push very hard, for people leaped aside to allow in his part of the drama, his authority.

John Frogget ushered him into the shooting gallery. Sammy Mack peered in after, holding the cloth aside. There was the partition with the cowboys painted on it, and a slot of the yellow light beyond, at the bottom of which a booted foot projected into view.

"Oh!" Dulcie crouched to my level and clutched me, and I clutched her around the neck in my fright. " 'Tis him, 'tis him!"

I had admired that boot in the Museum tent, to avoid looking further at his face as he took in the sight of us. "Hungry," I said, "that was the way he looked at us. I don't like to think

188

what is going through their minds when they look like that. But he was young, and not bad-looking, and dressed so fine!"

"He was doomed." Dulcie shivered. "I saw it. It was all over his palms, this possibility. It was all through his cards like a stain. When I see an outlay like that, I lie. Sometimes that averts it. I told him he would find love soon, and prosper in his business concerns, find peace in himself, all of that and more. Perhaps I babbled, and he saw the falsity in it. But I was only trying to help—oh!" She covered her mouth with her hand to stop more words falling out, doing their damage.

"Did you know the man, Dulcie?" Ugly Tom had seen our fright and come to us.

"You would have seen him, too, Tom," I said. "He spent an age among your babies and your three-headed lambs."

He looked startled, then disbelieving. "Oh, was he a young gentleman? Thin tie? Well-dressed? Little goatee?" He put up his hand to show how tall, and Dulcie and I nodded as if our heads were on the same string. "Well, I never!" He turned toward the shooting gallery, astonished. "You're right," he said to me, as if he had not noticed it himself, "he did spend a time with my exhibits. An inordinate amount of time."

"And with us outside, too, an ordinate amount," I said, holding Dulcie's neck tighter. "Back and forth, back and forth, *staring*. Which is why we are there, of course, so that people *may* stare. Did he say anything to you, Dulcie, that made you think he might—?"

She shook her head. "He gave me no clue. He didn't need to; it was all over his hands. I should have told him. *You're in terrible danger.* Perhaps if he knew that I saw—"

It was then that she walked by, toward the tent. It was not someone understandable, like The Lovely Zalumna. It was perfectly ordinary Fay Shipley, daughter of Cap Shipley, the head rigger.

I saw it as I'd seen the boot, when Sammy Mack opened the tent flap, and held it open longer than he needed. The world, the fates, whatever dooming powers there were that Dulcie sometimes saw the workings of before they acted, they conspired to show me, through the shiftings of the people in front of us, through the tent flap Sammy was gawking through, beside the partition, in the narrow slice of gallery, of world-in-itself, its sounds blotted out by the closer whispers and mutterings of bone-in-his-nose Tommy and Chan and Mrs. Em and the Wild Man and—

She hurried in, plain Fay Shipley. She stood beside the partition, her hands to her mouth. Then she lifted her head as someone approached her from inside, and—later I hated her for this—her arms loosened and lifted out to receive him, and as Sammy Mack dropped the canvas I saw John Frogget's forehead come to rest on her shoulder, John Frogget's arms encircle her waist, John Frogget's boot block my view of that other boot.

Then they both were gone. "Did you see that?" I said dazedly, in the cold, in the dark outside. "Fay and John Frogget?"

"Oh," said Dulcie. "Did you not know they were sweethearts?"

"Just freshly, just recent?"

"Oh no, months at least. Where have your eyes been?"

She stood then, away from me, and folded her arms up there. And Mrs. Em came running up to busybody, so it was all what-a-dreadful-thing and poor-John-Frogget awhile there, with every now and then a pause to allow me to exclaim to myself, *But I am prettier than Fay Shipley!*

And, *Look at my hair! When hers is so flat, as if she glued it down!*

And, *Why, I've never seen the girl laugh, to improve her looks that way!*

"What a thing to do on your last night, eh?" said Mrs. Em, with something of a giggle. "Come to the deadest night o' the circus, and look at freaks and specimens."

Oh, I was being so frivolous and vain, with the young gent dead in there, and why ever? "I don't know," I said. "*Is it so odd? What would you do, if you had killing yourself in mind?*"

"Would you have your fortune told?" said Dulcie wretchedly from on high. "To see whether you had the courage?"

"I think I am too ordinary," I said, surprised, staring at the tent flap.

Mrs. Em laughed. "That's no sin, child!"

"Oh, but I'm used to thinking how different I am from most people, how unusual. Yet this gentleman, and shooting himself in the eye . . . I don't know that I'd ever take my life in my own hands so. I wouldn't feel I had the right, you know? To such grand feelings, or even, to make such a mess, you know? Of someone else's floor, that would have to mop it up—"

"Ooh, he's more of a freak than you or I, dear," said Mrs. Em, right by my ear. Her stubby hand patted mine.

I folded mine away from her. I didn't want her coziness, her comforting me. I *wanted* to be grand and tragic; I wanted people to be awed by me as we were by the dead gentleman, not to say *How sweet!* and *But they are like little* dolls! *Flossie could pick one up, couldn't you, Floss?* I wanted to be tall, to have dignity, to shoot myself in the eye without it taking my whole arm's stretch to reach the trigger. I wanted to be all but invisible, too, until I did so, and to leave people wondering why I might have done it, instead of having them nod and say *Well, of course, she could expect no kind of normal life* as I lay freakish in my own blood on the floor, with my child boot sticking out my skirts.

"I'm going to ask Arthur, may I sit aboard his merry-go-round," I said.

"What, when a man has just died?" said Mrs. Em.

"I will not ask him to *spin* it," I said. "It will be safer. I will be out from underfoot, and it will cheer me up, and I will have a better view when they bring the body out."

"What a caution!" said Mrs. Em as I went.

I thrust myself in among skirts and trousers, painted legs and pantaloons, grass dresses and robe drapes. There is a privacy to being so small, a privacy and a permission—all children know it, and use it, and are forgiven. And "Oops!" and "Oh, I'm sorry,

Non" and "I say—oh, it's one of you!" people said as I forged a way through them, pushing aside their thighs and cloths and shadows.

And, finally, I forced through to the golden light of the merry-go-round. The animals were stiff on their posts, and empty-saddled, that ought to glide and spin, and lift and lower their riders; the pootling, piping music was stilled.

"Arthur," I commanded the ticket man nearby, a rag hanging from his pocket smudged with the grease of the roundabout's workings. "Lift me up onto a pony, before someone treads me into the mud!"

Which he did with a will, for people enjoy to be ordered by dwarves as they like to be ordered by children, up to a point. And there in the golden glow I sat high-headed, above the hats and feathers and turbans of the ghoulish crowd turned away from me. I wished the light were as warm as it looked; I wished the music were filling my ears. I dreamed—hard, as if the vehemence of my dreaming would make it happen—that my shiny black horse would surge forward beneath me, and that I would be spun away from this place and this night, lifted and lowered instead past Lake Geneva, past Constantinople, past Windermere and Tokyo Palace and Gay Paree, past Geneva again, and the Lake, again and again around the whole picturesque, giltframed world, for as long as ever I needed.

# Eyelids of the Dawn

Iтсну. Тнат was the тноuGнt that woke me, woke my hearing, woke my skins and mind. Threw a strong light, constant as if electric powered, back down my memory.

Louse itch, mite itch. They have been at me all day. For many days and evenings, certainly, but this day is freshest to me. All my terrazzo and my faux parquetry is tapped and scuffed by their shoes, streaked with their dropped food, rolled on by their children's tantrums and strollers. This is what happens when the doors of your face are opened: the lice crowd in. When the light goes, their business is finished, and they crowd out again, and leave only their itch behind.

It is all through my pipes and columns, this itch. The lice are the source of it, but it grows in places where they have not been, away from the thoroughfares, shop rooms and restrooms and workrooms, escalators and lifts: in drains with other vermin, in germ-scummed sewer pipes; evaporating from my roofs' trays and gutters. All along my steel, between the steel and the concrete it strengthens, gnawing here, making me twitch there.

I have so many seams where it can gather. Impervious to air, I am, a sealed unit with my own climate, but inside and out I am all corners, all niches and crevices, false walls and cavities. I have my glossy rooms and my disinfected, but parts of me are never seen and never polished, never swept or wiped or flicked with rag or feather duster. Much of me is only ever rinsed by rain; much of me goes untouched, and some of me is buried in dirt. Worms weave around my feet, rats run about my ankles, some small thing putrefies in a back corner of me.

And all around me in the night, they are still there, the lice, crawling in the other blocks, roosting, feeding, squabbling, ceaseless. Dogs trot the streets and cattle wander; rats run; more lice live there, the sort that wait in the day at the doors of my face and importune the others entering and leaving. And on their skins and the dogs' and the rats' and the cattle's, louse-vermin crawl and bite and bother, so that the lice twitch an ear, or scratch a leg, or rub themselves against a post or building, to relieve their own minuscule itches.

Overhead—it is insufferable!—the million sky mites shine, fastened all across the heavens, their fat queen moving among them full of eggs, full of young. Their mandibles are sunk in the sky flesh, and they hang, and suck, and suck, and crawl about, night to night, slowed by the weight of sky blood they have drunk.

# Eyelids of the Dawn

Limb and limb, support and strut of me—the itch is bad now in this sector and now in that. First my waters tickle me, all their suspended pestilence; next the stale chilled air in my ducts, listless against the furry vents, the black-rimmed vanes of fans, strokes me with its dusts and damps; next it is the strips of the pulled-down roll doors, their blindness, their blurring plastic slatted-ness; then the emptiness vibrates, the very space; then the litter of louse signage, and the bower after bower of sleeping offerings, unoffered, ready to be offered tomorrow.

A breeze begins, beyond me; it is the first weather I appreciate, though memory tells me I have baked in strong sunshine, borne up under long rains, conducted lightnings through myself into the earth below where they belong. This light, soft thing, though, this breath, opens pores all over my impermeables: my glass, my pebblecrete, my metal, my silicon. My asphalt and plastics all wake in it and register: where this breeze comes from, there is refreshment, and absence of all the crawlers and biters whose clawfalls and wheel stripes and tickling wings bother me, whose tails drag across me thin and leathery, whose whiskers brush and toes stub and spittle stars me, whose hairs powder down, or drop in sheaves and spiral locks, and are never quite all swept away. All *through* me hair snips, hair dust, dust of all things, worm frass and beetle dung and flakes of skin and scab shift in the drafts. I shudder, and loosen one footing in the ground.

I will have to discard some underparts, I think. All this heavy stuff where the louse carriers install themselves, all this cement work that is not really mall, but only ancillary to mall, all that can go, can be dropped away.

The loosening takes some work and time; I am stiff from my long sleep in the one position; I am unaccustomed; and my materials are not so flexible as louse muscle, all oiled and made supple by bloods and waters. I don't mind the work; from the breath of the breeze I can tell how far I need to travel; the night is long, if I remember right, and I have time.

When I am loosened, I draw up my limbs—which are all walking limbs, none of those pick-and-manipulators lice have, that they handle things with, their desires and their treasures and each other—and themselves, too, picking their noses, scratching their ears, moving their hairs about. I draw my walkers up and with great pain and concentration accomplish the uncoupling, and in many cases the breaking, from all that needs detaching below. The carriage places fall away well, for they were not strongly constructed; like folded, stacked stock cartons they pile on themselves in their hole, and I can refoot myself on them and force upward, and snap the stubborner pipe joints, the stretchier cords, the cables. The pain is refreshing after the itches; some of my irritations flow out of me with the wastewater, with the released sewage; some of them puff away on the breeze with the hissing gas from the main I crushed in my heavings.

I put my face doors up and search the air with my clearer pores. There it is, that fresher level, that sweeter, without shit in it or breath or burps of lice, without their sweat pong or their sick smell or the odor of their linted or fungused crevices, or of their decaying teeth. I turn myself about on the ruins, face into the breeze and set off.

Sendra counted the hours; she was so tired she had to count them on her fingers: eight to eleven, then an hour and a half while Nuri fussed and refused to settle, then forty-five minutes and Nuri's nightmare, twenty more minutes after that before the neighbor boy came home, singing and banging and being scolded by his uncle, then another. Altogether, no more than four and a half hours yet. All she would be able to think of to-morrow was how much she would rather be sleeping.

She paused by the window. Nuri readied himself to complain his way out of sleep, so she turned, jogging and shushing him, back to the room full of corners and obstacles and soft darkness, to the path she had cleared for herself between the stacked laundry and the boxed Turkish ovens they were minding for Veddi's brother's venture.

In the hall she rocked from foot to foot. Veddi's breathing came out one door and the broken-pipe-and-soap smell flowed out the other. Together with the hour of night they made a grainy soup of darkness, unbreathable for Sendra, unbearable.

She fought her way free of it, crossed the cluttered room to the window again, and leaned her shoulder and pressed the corner of her forehead on the cool, gritty glass.

A slice of city, she could see; three lit windows, close, far and very far, and between them specks of street lighting and a moving taxi lantern. Not so long ago she would have seen those windows and thought, *What is behind them? Night owls dreaming great literatures, freed from the day's distractions? Beautiful women pining for their absent men? Insomniacs scrubbing, sorting, reading?* Always she imagined them solitary, compelled by their own desires or diseases. Now she knew that they were all slaves, their masters tiny monsters like Nuri, in their wrappings, in the fitfulness and fancy of their sleeping. Exhaustion pressed like an iron bar across all their brows, lined their bones, leadened their blood so that when they sat down they could barely imagine rising. When they lay, listening to the renewed squirm and whimpering of the baby across the room, they lay under exhaustion's weight, and the rage boiled up in them, and there was nothing they could do about it, there was nowhere they could let it out.

What?

Strange.

Sendra was used to waking, already half out of bed, to the sound of Nuri's little cough, Nuri's little drawing of breath for a cry. But now she stood motionless, back from the window, her head lowered and peering, entirely alert and wondering whether she had dreamed that sound. It was as if the very earth itself had coughed, just quietly, coming awake. All was silent now; all was still outside except that taxi lamp—which had wobbled, had it not?, at the sound, at the movement, but now sailed on.

Nuri lay silent at her breast, attached but no longer sucking. Sendra felt a great fear. Her duty in the night was to keep Nuri from waking Veddi, who had the daytime job that kept the three of them housed and fed. Was it also her business, then, to keep the whole earth quiet for Veddi? How was she to quieten the outside for him? How could she pick up and settle the world?

No, it was the night hour, making her think such things, magnifying sounds and sensations. She had fallen to sleep a tiny instant, that was all, and dreamed that moment of startlement. The floor, the wall, the window, they had not really trembled; only Sendra herself had.

But there it came again: a deep uncertainty, a tearing underfoot like roots of some vast plant pulling free, a ticking of the windowpane.

The woken piece of earth arrived, between the far and the very far window light. It might only have been shadow, some trick of cloud and moon, except for the sensations of its arrival, the drags and thuds of its steps—though these, like the voices of elephants and the harbingers of earthquakes, happened only at the very lowest edge of hearing, might not truly be happening at all. It bulked in the slot of city between Capri Towers and the government offices, blotting out the view of the square, starlit roofs like steps up to the distant hills. It blotted out those hills, and the lower stars, with its peaks and corners. It reared and sank, slowly, weightily, as a piece of the earth should.

It passed behind the offices. It was gone; the view was as it had been—stars, hills, three lit windows—although the deep rumbling, the scraping, continued awhile. Sendra watched the top of the offices, in case it should rise there, turn and approach and endanger her. But on it went and away. She stood, still watching, still watching nothing, in the silence it left, awake to her very finger and toe tips, with Nuri a sleeping stone in her arms.

Figuro whistled along the street, his last few bottles chiming white in the float behind him. His job was to bring the morning, a mass of cold white light from which he broke pieces, to deliver them to people's doorsteps, a clot of sunlight here, a blob of cool dawn there. And only when he had dispensed the last light globe from the float on the last round was the real sun, so vulgar and huge and hot, allowed to come up and begin its business.

Figuro was half-mad, and people complained about his whistling, which woke them when they had just fallen asleep from coming off shift. They said their baby startled awake when his float took the drainway in front of their house, and jangled all suddenly. "He drives like a boy racer," they cried. "What is his hurry?"

"Flatten out your street, then," said Job the dairy boss, "or stuff rags in your ears. I don't care what." For Figuro was half-sane as well, and the sane half of him was the perfect milk-delivering machine, an extension of the little three-wheel float with the walleyed cow painted across its back. Other milkmen came—out of nowhere, with references—and went—into gambling or drunkenness or, sometimes, who knew where they went? They did not show and they did not show, and then Job must find another. While these men churned past him, Figuro stayed stolid and reliable at the center of High-Minded Milk Incorporation, and if the flowers beyond the nuns' hedge top sang to the man, or the cats chattered, or there were three houses Figuro could not deliver to because of their frightening faces, none of this bothered Job.

Figuro himself did not mind, either, about any such complaining or unpopularity. He was fixed in his methods and sunny in his disposition; he was intent on lighting the way into the day, with these two milk lamps to number 29 with the shoe scraper, and this one-cream-one-milk to number 31, where the tassels of the hall rug straggled out under the door as if pleading with him: *Help me escape! Help! I am trapped and trampled all the livelong day!*

He laughed on 31's step. "Foolish!" he said. "You do not know when you are on a lucky wicket, do you?" And laughing he went back to the little purring home on three wheels, its light diminished by half now. He rattled and released it into movement and on they went, he and the beast and the remaining bottles. The stars sang their thin song above, and one window squared up gold with twitching curtains while another blinked out to join the dark surrounding wall.

The stars had begun to be erased, gradually covered wash by wash by the upswimming grayness of predawn, when Figuro cut his engine for the last reload at the depot, and then cut it again, or tried to. But the engine noise did not stop as it ought.

He stood back and regarded the float disappointedly. Things should behave as they always did; they should not make difficulties; they should not ask for new stratagems from him. The float sat there paling in the coming dawn, becoming more and more its battered daily self, losing its beastness and its magic.

A darkness swung in the sky. Another darkness pushed across and covered the first. Beyond the float some kind of door slammed down, and the float tipped away from Figuro toward it. He swayed to keep his footing. The door flexed—rough, dark, crusted—and was gone, flailing upward into the thundercloud, the mother ship, the shaggy black belly passing over.

It rained on him: clots of clayey soil, balled-up sweet wrappers, fragments of mirror glass and concrete. The rain bounced and tinkled on the depot float-park while the thing blacked out all but the edges of the sky, all but the very fringe of what little light there had been.

Figuro was accustomed to not understanding. He stood in the shadow and waited, untroubled, for all the impressions to come together into sense, or perhaps not. Gusts of troubled air swiped at him, rattled the leaning float and the depot gates.

He ought to be afraid of it, perhaps. No other milkmen were here yet to show him how much danger he was in, to run about and drag him by the arm: *Inside, simpleton!* Only Figuro stood in the broken black field of asphalt, his tipped float somehow reproving him, and the thing, the storm, the aircraft, continuing overhead.

With a final spatter of its sand-and-stony rain it dragged its back end, waving threads and shiny tubes of tail, away over the plant, over High-Minded's administration building with its cozy offices that Figuro had never seen, with its unsuspecting pediments and corbels and much-divided windows, now mirroring this star to that again, this crying seagull to that.

All around, the grit and gobbets were scattered on the tar like assorted jewels. Figuro could do nothing for the float; several men would be needed to lift it out; several men were not here to help him.

So he followed. Eastward, the thing had gone, toward the water, toward the light. He felt an inclination that way himself, most mornings, but dutifully back into the streets he always went, delivering.

He rounded the corner into Munificent Way and he could see it, its edge proceeding above the buildings, swaying in such a way he could not tell how many legs it had. Certainly more than an elephant, quite a different rhythm. He hurried, he ran, because while it gave every impression of slow, considered progress, it was shrinking in his eye. And another part of Figuro was caught up as a child is caught by a circus parade or a brass band or, yes, a string of elephants single file, as if such things had a wake into which unthinking beings were drawn, without their particularly choosing.

Figuro was a thin man, but he had not run for a long time and he took a little while to establish a gait he could sustain. Above and ahead the hems of the creature moved on away; here below raced his mismanaged breath, and his unaccustomed legs, rubbering and paining and tiring. He willed the thing to stay in sight. He didn't speak or call to it as once he might have—since his mother had died he obeyed her better than he ever had, and one of the things she had insisted was that tools and buildings and anything that you could not see had ears you did not address.

Now he saw the sea, the dark line of it through the railing beyond the paler stripe of empty highway. Now he smelt it over the other smells, muted as they were by morning's coolness—the splashy salt smell of play, of childhood. Now he heard it, beyond his own breaths and grunts, its thin collapsements on the shore beside the unawakened town. And he was out on the highway, and he could see the whole creature.

It brought the last several of its leg pairs, leg trios, over the railing after itself, while its jagged chin thrust out over the first shallows like a king's sea palace.

And palace it was, or at least architecture, Figuro saw clearly. It was made all of slabs and brittle stuff that ought not to move, and yet it had got something of sinew into itself, and something of flexible skin, something of a head—he wished he could see the face that belonged to this outreaching being, this clumsy animal, this great ugly child. Perhaps even it had ears, and if he went up close it would hear him. Perhaps he could help.

He ran straight across the highway, bent and stepped through the railing to the grassed area beyond. His joints were grateful for earth instead of paving; he had energy again with the creature-that-was-a-building in his sights, arrayed across the view and so unusual. He was glad his mother was gone; he would not have to describe the impossible thing to her. He could just see it and have it go unexplained, un-made-sense-of, wondrous.

He ran. He wished it would turn this way. "Hi!" he cried, and "Hey!", and he leaped and waved trying to make himself big enough to catch its eye.

Of course it did not see or hear him—or if it did, he was not important to it. Caterpillar-like it assembled its segments, hunching the shoulderish ones at the fore, sorting and shuffling the ones behind.

Then it shook its head—not monstrously, not cavalierly, but as if gathering courage before going to an interview with the High-Minded Milk boss, for instance. Momentarily it had a mane, and shards flew out of it, some black, some only flashes of beginning dawn light, long triangles in the sky and then gone into the briefly furred sea surface.

And into the water it walked. It was the wonderfullest thing. Figuro ran to the edge of the grass, scrambled down the slope of cemented rocks and stood, up to his ankles in the soft, cold sand. He struggled a few steps forward, but without the spring of grass his legs were uninterested, and his eyes were so busy—his mouth was open as if it could see, too—that he did not fight to force himself onward.

Anyway, he wanted this view of all of it, and to hear the creaks and grindings from its whole length, poppings and thumps. Besides, see all the stuff falling from its sides and undersides! If he went too close he could be speared, crushed, blinded by some small flying-off thing.

"Oh!" He clasped his hands and shook them up at the thing. "You are a marvel!"

Its forelegs sank in the soft watered sand and lifted, and sank again. On and in it went, still with its back end progressing across the grass. It breasted the little waves, breaking their ration of dawn sheen into an unshining white splashiness. It was clumsy, of course, clumsier than a horse or elephant, meeting the water for the first-ever time and accustoming itself to its own shape against the water forces, the thickness and the wave beats and the more tidal changes. It lumbered. Expecting the floor to be as flat as the city's, it slumped and huffed and surged in surprise at the slope; it stumbled. Its underneath splatted wide sprays out to the sides and front. It seemed to fall to its knees, all its different sets of knees, one after another, floundering and slanting and gathering itself up to try again, as if it fled, rather than sought its right place.

But there, the back end of it was now over the sea rim, and the front was shouldered well in, up to the eyebrows maybe—Figuro wished he could see. Spray flew up off the front edge and onto the roof. Would it float? Figuro hoped it would finish as something like a crocodile, just the top of it snaking its lumps and spines away into the sunrise, the legs working invisibly below.

The first water swirled pink and silver across the roof. Figuro was disappointed to see it, but still he had to admit that it was beautiful, it was right, just as when you washed yourself in the sacred river you had to immerse yourself completely, not merely splash water up onto your head top but go right down, hold your breath and be part of the river for a moment. Figuro had opened his eyes under there, seen the pale misty water and the brown level of stirred-up mud, and his Uncle Pooti's trousers flapping in the current as in a strong wind full of dust.

Down so went this creature entirely, piece by blockish piece, following itself ungainly into the sea. And behind its last legs and trailing tails, Figuro ran back and forth at the water's edge, his cries lost in the sluicings of the shallows, in the up-bubbling blasts of air and wreckage. The mystery muttered against the sea bottom; on the surface it left a slick path, edged with ragged fountains, from Figuro to the new sun a bright peck mark out of the horizon, from the new sun a golden fingernail, across all of the sea, to the milkman running on the shore.

I reach the edge of the world. There are no lice here, and no louse carriages. Soft fur strokes my sore torn paws, and then even softer stuff, a kind of cloud-ground. It gives somewhat before holding, relenting.

Out there beyond are two skies, both shining full of hope. The gentlest color creeps upon the upper one, color of Ladies' Underwear, and with a lace of clouds there, yes, a trim, *accents*. The same kind shade swims upon the water, cresting its night darkness, spilling forward on its foam.

# Yellowcake

I step off into space, all itching. It's cold, the morning, the water. It clings close in my crevices; it climbs up my outsides and into the lower beginnings of my innards, the first rooms there and the cavities; it soothes the broken places; it lifts the grit and grain off me. The loose pieces wag and break off and are gone from their dangling and banging.

Ah! I open my face. It rushes in, the morning, the light, the universe, the cleansing sea. I sink into the relief and it laps and laves me all around, hurries across the top of me to cover me, and rushes and spurts in all my compartments, soaking and floating the disordered goods there, dousing the memories of my electronica, pouring ruin along my walkways, tossing and tumbling my shelves, my stacks, my storerooms of louse ephemera.

Down farther I sink, quite covered now, quite gone from the world's sight, from the world's crawlings. Collected airs bleed upward through me; gouts and threads of bubble stream lightward. Everything is blurred here and stirring; every sound is muffled and closed in; the hollows resound differently, deeperly; nothing is sudden. Temperatures trail slow strings across my face, and softness sucks below. Rocks crack my underparts over themselves; growths lie down and make matting for my wounded belly.

I lie, all my itches gone or going, shifting this wing or that corridor to blub up a bubble, to complete my skin of cool, of wet, to drown the last louse traces, any eggs they might have left, any irritants. Around me the vast blur moves, out and empty of those scraping creatures and those squalling. Instead come smoother others, moving without benefit of flooring, arriving on the slow treacly winds of the sea, eyeing me, kissing and nibbling my surfaces, rolling into my foyers and uncoiling, shy upon my travertine and my piled, sharded glass. I lie and breathe of the free-moving tides, and let the sea beasts have the run of me.

There was too much sky altogether, thought Sendra, stepping out onto Commercial Row. Too much sky and too much wall and pavement—where had everyone gone?

It was so quiet that she heard her own gasp twice—once from her mouth and again bounced back to her from the shop fronts opposite, a tiny moment later. Commercial Row was long and wide, inviting your eye, your feet, to wander. But today it didn't end as it should, at the shining promise of Chumley Mall. Gone were the chrome and glass doors three times man-height holding in the cooled air, the giant billboard faces with their intimate smiles, the ant people passing in and out. Today only sky filled the street end, and the inconsequential buildings beyond where the mall ought to be, and on the ground a crowd milling, excitement, indeed like stirred-up ants.

Slowly she walked toward the difference. It was as if her own head had suddenly changed shape; it was as if someone important had died—had anyone died? Would she see dreadful things? Still she walked. Nuri was tied onto her back, like goods, silent and warm, and she was a grown-up now; she was a mother, and she could bear anything; she could look any horror in the face.

Slowly the nothing approached her, towering and teetering

emptied sky, with a fuss, a froth, of people below. She stood a little way back from them, catching between their heads and movements glimpses of torn earth, of a pipe gushing, concrete slabs stacked, or leaning in the clay crater-sides.

A tiny old woman was brought out of the crowd by her scolding daughter: "Well, by heaven, the suit is gone now, isn't it? Gone to smithereens along with the rest. Come, Mama. I need a cup of tea, I am so shocked."

"How can it be?" said the old woman, bewildered. "All that explosion, and yet it woke no one. Nobody heard a thing."

All sounds fell silent to Sendra then, although the mama and others continued to mouth, and a vehicle, a small type of digging machine, parted the crowd almost at Sendra's elbow. The night silence clutched her close, and the machine's trundling reminded her feet of the apartment floor last night, of being bare and tired by the window.

She pushed through the crowd behind the machine. When it turned right she went left, and found the concrete apron everyone used to cross to reach the cool of Chumley Mall. Beyond its broken far edge the ground gaped, the ground yawned, a muddy mouth full of broken teeth, broken gray biscuit, and tubes and piping slumped or poked cockily up, fountaining wires or dribbling water. On the far rim of the crater all the town's levels of wealth were lined up in order, from the white Shogun Apartments with their flags at the hilltop, down to the woven-walled huts and lean-tos along the river's filth.

Right before her eyes men put up a barrier, a wire fence that broke up the crater view into diamonds. People pushed around her and clustered to the wire, hooking their fingers in, and some of the children their toes. Sendra was glad of them, that they hid the crater again, that they began to fill the great befurred silence it had been yelling forth with their exclamations, the children with their questions, and everyone with their ordinariness—a man eating a banana as he stared through the wire, a child or two sidling up with their begging faces on.

Sendra pushed back, so as not to be wedged at the front of the crowd. She was on Commercial Row again, walking away from everyone, with nowhere to go now, her market bag loose in her hand. "I dreamt it," she said to the empty street. The paving and the litter passed her eyes unseen. The memory of the woken thing lumped up out of the possible. Her foot soles crawled with its wrenchings, with its breakings, with its pullings free.

# Acknowledgments

I thank the following people in particular for their help and support: Simon Spanton of Gollancz for championing *Black Juice* in the UK; Jonathan Strahan for his efficiency and straight dealing as an editor; Sharyn November for accepting "Ferryman" almost before I sent it; Nancy Siscoe for putting forward the possibility of adding some loving-kindness to this collection, in response to which I wrote "Into the Clouds on High," which is published here for the first time; and Kathy Gollan for the conversation that gave "Into the Clouds on High" its final form.

# Publication History

The stories in this collection first appeared in the publications listed below.

"The Point of Roses," in *Black Juice*. London: Gollancz, 2006.

"The Golden Shroud," in *Picture This 2*. Edited by Annabel Smith and Helen Chamberlin. Melbourne: Pearson Education, 2009.

"A Fine Magic," in *Eidolon I*. Edited by Jonathan Strahan and Jeremy G. Byrne. Perth, Western Australia: Eidolon Books, 2006.

"An Honest Day's Work," in *The Starry Rift*. Edited by Jonathan Strahan. New York: Firebird, 2008.

"Night of the Firstlings," in *Eclipse Two*. Edited by Jonathan Strahan. San Francisco: Night Shade Books, 2008.

"Catastrophic Disruption of the Head," in *Tales from the Tower, The Willful Eye*. Edited by Isobelle Carmody and Nan McNab. Crows Nest, New South Wales: Allen & Unwin, 2011.

"Ferryman," in *Firebirds Soaring*. Edited by Sharyn November. New York: Firebird, 2009.

"Living Curiosities," in *Sideshow: Ten Original Tales of Freaks, Illusionists, and Other Matters Odd and Magical*. Edited by Deborah Noyes. Somerville, MA: Candlewick Press, 2009.

"Eyelids of the Dawn," in *New Australian Stories*. Edited by Aviva Tuffield. Melbourne: Scribe, 2009.

The Literature Board of the Australia Council for the Arts, the Australian Government's arts funding and advisory body, funded my writing with a fellowship in 2006–2007, during which time many of these stories were written.

# Where the Stories Started

These stories were inspired, as far as I can recall, in the following ways.

"The Point of Roses" started when two things came together in my head: the BBC documentary *Gypsy Wars*, about the community response to Gypsies in Cottenham, Cambridgeshire; and my nephew Finn inventing the verb "to pumft," and naming a soft-toy dog he owned Pumfter von Schnitzel.

The whole point of Pearson Education's *Picture This* anthologies was to show school students how stories could grow from visual images. The picture they sent me to work from was of a stone stairway in what I took to be a castle interior. I'm not sure how Rapunzel's hair managed to animate itself, but as soon as I saw it unlocking the door of the prince's cell, I had "The Golden Shroud."

"A Fine Magic" started off with a note to myself: *a carousel made of ice*. Also with my attraction to the word "fascinator," used in the sense of a person who fascinates or bewitches people.

"An Honest Day's Work" was inspired by a documentary about shipbreaking in Bangladesh—there have been several of these, and I couldn't tell you which it was. When I did some follow-up research, I found Edward Burtynsky's photographs of the Chittagong shipbreaking yards to be a further spur to the writing. These can be found at edwardburtynsky.com (follow the links PROJECTS—›Shipbreaking).

"Night of the Firstlings" happened when I first heard Paul Kelly's song "Passed Over" on his album *Foggy Highway*.

"Catastrophic Disruption of the Head" was written when Isobelle Carmody and Nan McNab asked me to modernize a fairy tale for their *Tales from the Tower* anthology. The big-eyed dogs in Hans Christian Andersen's "The Tinderbox" had always bothered me, but when I went back to read it, I found the whole tale full of disturbing material I wanted to explore.

"Ferryman" sprang fully formed from my reading a little article called "The River Ferry," written by Harrison Fridd, eight-year-old son of a ferryman, of Waikerie, South Australia, and published in *Living Landscapes: Writing and Art by Children of the Murray-Darling Basin* (Primary English Teaching Association/ Murray-Darling Basin Commission, Marrickville and Canberra, 2005).

"Living Curiosities" came from the same source as my junior novel *Walking Through Albert* (Allen & Unwin). I can't remember where I read or heard about the idea that ghostly events play themselves out over and over again, like video loops but with added gooseflesh, but it's prompted three stories already and it still isn't worn out. Also, walking past Bullens Lane in central Melbourne, I started thinking about a character who was Circus personified (Bullen's Circus toured Australia from the 1920s to the 1960s), and who hid himself away in just such a lane during the winter months.

"Eyelids of the Dawn" grew out of my commuting by train through Burwood in Sydney's inner west and looking across to Burwood Plaza, seeing how big it was and how uncomfortable it looked crouched there among all the other shops and houses. Visiting Chennai (as part of the Asialink Literature Touring Program 2007) and walking from the Park Hotel to Marina Beach on our first afternoon in India, and later seeing Spencer Plaza, added significant detail to the story.

Photo © Steven Dunbar

**Margo Lanagan** is a highly acclaimed writer of novels and short stories. Her novels include *The Brides of Rollrock Island* and *Tender Morsels*, which received a Michael L. Printz Honor Award and won the World Fantasy Award for Best Novel. Her short-story collection *Black Juice* also received a Printz Honor and won two World Fantasy Awards (Best Collection and Best Short Story). Her other story collections include *Red Spikes* and *White Time*.

Margo lives in Sydney, Australia.

# Discover Margo Lanagan's latest novel

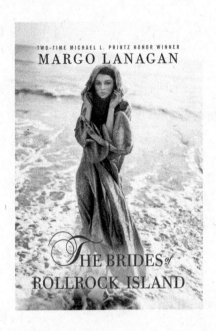

★ "Lanagan's world is busily, passionately alive.
Seal, human, sea, sky, and the rocks themselves
animate this powerful story."
—*The Horn Book Magazine*, Starred

*Turn the page to read an excerpt.*

"Come to Fisher's! They've found a mermaid! Come and look!"

Bee stood out from the step to stop them. "A mermaid? But the boats did not go out today!"

"She walked into town, with not a stitch on!" cried Hex Scupper. He ran on, then called back over his shoulder, "Up from Crescent Corner!"

"A mermaid!" Bee exclaimed after them.

I hid the shaking of my hands in my apron. "What can they mean? Perhaps it is only some kind of malformed fish."

"A fish that walked into town?"

"Let us go and see, then."

I went to Mam's doorway, pulling on my coat. "What're *you* want?" she said. "Fetch that daughter of mine."

"I am off down Fisher's a moment, to see a sea-girl," I said. "I will lock you in, just in case you take a mind to follow me."

She glared and did not know me still—her knowing had come and gone a great deal lately. I could talk nonsense to her, or insult her outright, and she would forget a moment after.

I locked the door and Bee and I set off for Fisher's, falling in with a crowd of others who spilled from their doors, donning coats and pulling on shawls. I was glad of Bee, for she could take care of the talking—which she did, for along with all the other betrothed or married women, she had a great deal of anxiety to spill out, about this mermaid. I went quietly among them, nodding at what they said and making the right faces so as not to be noticed.

We met Doris Shingle, coming up. "Aye, she's fair," she said. "Fair strange, you ask me. Foreign-looking—as you'd expect, I suppose, for she's not of this country."

"Has she seaweed hair?" joked Abby Staines. "Has she sucker-fingers like an octopus?"

"None of that," said Doris. "Her sea-ness is quite gone. She's fingers like you or me, only finer. And her hair is finer too, and as straight as if you took and ironed it."

Pensive men we met too, who would not be drawn so much. Their silence did nothing to improve the wives' tempers.

Then we were at Fisher's. They had put the sea-girl in his back room there; two doors led to it from the main store, and the whole town was filing in one and out the other very slowly. Those coming out were some of them eager to tell us everything we were about to see; others sidled away, or went head down, and would not be pressed. The ones that did speak each had a different story—she was fair enough, she was ugly, she was the fairest thing ever made; her hair was like silk cloth, like rats' tails, like a horse's floppy mane; she was sulky, she smiled like an angel, she was the most radiant creature; she had swum from Spain, she was clearly of the sea, she had nothing about her of the underwater. I hardly knew what to expect when finally I pushed and shuffled into the back room with the others.

Fisher's women had got the poor thing into a dress, but it

did not fit her well; its puffed sleeves sat sadly out from her shoulders, and her long shins dangled below the hem, with the fine small bare feet that looked as if they would not hold anything up of substance. In the window light her skin had a greenish cast, and the dress was a particular yellow that set it off badly.

"She looks *ill*," Hatty Marchant whispered to someone, behind my shoulder.

I was crowded along by those eager to enter, everyone breathing and murmuring. Mag Fisher was seated by the girl, looking about fiercely.

"Has she a voice like us?" someone ventured at last from behind me.

"I've a voice," said the sea-girl, and I heard that clear enough. Her voice was low, and of course lovely, and held an accent of some kind, I thought. I wanted immediately to hear it again, to make sure.

"Will she be staying?"

"That's enough of questions," snapped Mag. "I've answered everything over and over. Go and ask those who already know. I won't have the girl badgered."

"We're not badgering *her*, Mag. We're badgering *you*." A wicked titter ran among us.

This was how it would be, then: the women pretending this was everyday, that she was not much of a girl to look at, while her enchantment went to work upon the men. I could see it, their eyes fixing and following the length of her hair, of her limbs, of her slimness under the awful dress, their lips parting. I began to see the size of what I'd accomplished that evening at the Crescent. What chance did these men have against my faceless, heartless periwinkle girl? Poor defenseless fools. And poor wives and mothers! They were no more than encumbrances now. They could titter and screech and weep as much as they liked, in the weeks and months to come. They would not be paid any mind.

Was she beautiful, the sea-maid? *Fair strange*, Doris had said, and I thought that was a fine assessment. I had seen her face before, of course, or very like it: the portrait in Strangleholds' attic, the Spanish dancers on my brother's postcard. Their hair, like hers, was neat dark wings either side of their faces; their eyebrows too were drawn clear-edged against skin that bore not a freckle or a fleck. This girl's eyes, like those others', were wide and dark; her hands were long, the fingers slender and longer than the palms. Her mouth was like my own, only beautiful; looking upon it I could see why whoever-it-was had asked could it speak, for it seemed to be made only for people to admire, for ornament: curve-edged, bruise-colored, plump, heavy. I looked about me at the small mouths, hardly lipped at all, spattered with freckles, little pinch slots into the women's worried, or disagreeable, or frankly afraid faces. Any man seeing this maiden's lips would want to lay kisses on them; he would want to roll in the cushions of those lips, swim the depths of those eyes, run his hands down the long foreign lengths of this girl. Oh, I thought, women of Rollrock, you are *nothing* now.